Willa
and the
Whale

OTHER BOOKS

By Chad Morris & Shelly Brown

Mustaches for Maddie

Squint

By Chad Morris

Cragbridge Hall, book 1:
The Inventor's Secret

Cragbridge Hall, book 2:
The Avatar Battle

Cragbridge Hall, book 3:
The Impossible Race

By Shelly Brown

Ghostsitter

Willa
and the
Whale

CHAD MORRIS AND SHELLY BROWN

SHADOW
MOUNTAIN

To all the amazing mothers in the world, including ours.
You make the world better.

Emoji icon on page 99 by ya_blue_ko/Shutterstock.com
Other interior images by Oko Laa, Stock09, Goran J, ntnt/Shutterstock.com

Visit us at shadowmountain.com

All characters in this book are fictitious, and any resemblance to actual persons, living or dead, is purely coincidental.

Library of Congress Cataloging-in-Publication Data
Names: Morris, Chad, author. | Brown, Shelly, 1979– author.
Title: Willa and the whale / Chad Morris and Shelly Brown.
Description: Salt Lake City : Shadow Mountain, [2020] | Audience: Ages 12+. | Audience: Grades 4–6. | Summary: "Twelve-year-old Willa, grieving the loss of her mother, a renowned marine biologist, discovers she can talk to whales"— Provided by publisher.
Identifiers: LCCN 2019038783 | ISBN 9781629727318 (hardback)
Subjects: CYAC: Whales—Fiction. | Human-animal communication—Fiction. | Mothers and daughters—Fiction. | Grief—Fiction.
Classification: LCC PZ7.M827248 Wi 2020 | DDC [Fic]—dc23
LC record available at https://lccn.loc.gov/2019038783

Printed in the United States of America
Lake Book Manufacturing, Melrose Park, IL

10 9 8 7 6 5 4 3 2 1

CHAPTER 1

Trained by the Best

Willa Twitchell, Journal #2, three years ago

Yesterday at school, Nolan Rossi made fun of my whale drawings and called me an ocean freak. When I said he was a basketball freak, he said at least basketball was important. What? I like basketball, but it isn't nearly as important as the ocean. The ocean covers 70% of the earth's surface. Basketball courts don't even cover 1%. The ocean helps regulate the temperature of the earth. The ocean provides the main source of protein to more than a billion people. And I bet Nolan knows nothing about the amount of important medicines that we have found over the years in the sea. And who knows if we might find a cure for cancer down there. Plus, there are creatures and mysteries in the ocean we haven't even discovered yet.

That's why my mom once said, "The ocean is filled

with more wonders than the most brilliant explorer could ever discover or fully appreciate." And she should know; she's a brilliant marine biologist.

But that's not even the best part. After she said that, she looked at me and said, "Just like you." She compared me to the ocean, filled with wonders. I loved it.

Nobody compares the people they love to basketball. That's just weird. Ocean wins. Take that, Nolan Rossi.

~~~~~~~~~~~~~~~~~~~~~~~~~

A whale surfaced, rolled on its back, and slapped the water with one of its huge fins. Gallons and gallons of ocean splashed up when a flipper the length of a car slammed down against it.

Perfect. It was like the whale knew that I needed to see it today.

"That was a humpback," I called out, leaning against the railing and filming on my phone. This was going to be one of the best shots I'd taken in twelve years. Well, I'm not sure I can say that, being twelve, and knowing that I didn't take wildlife pictures in the first few years; I couldn't even wipe my own nose. But it was going to be really, really good.

"Probably," my dad said, scratching his beard, "I'm not quite sure." I guess he thought I asked him if it was a humpback. As if I couldn't recognize one on my own. I'd know those bumps along the fins anywhere. He wasn't really paying attention. Classic Dad. He wasn't like me. I came to be here, to surge up and crash down with the waves, to search the endless blue for a sign of something amazing, to experience it. Just like I'd been taught. And I especially needed it today. Dad knew that. That's why he brought me.

We had enough bad in our lives and it was time for something good. Something remarkable. Like a thirty-three-ton whale doing acrobatics out of the water. But Dad kept trying to talk to me about the bad stuff instead of enjoying the nature show. Terrible idea. It was like taking a kid to Disneyland for a long, deep emotional conversation.

Over my twelve years, I have seen so many sea creatures: dolphins, starfish, seahorses, crabs, whales, marlins, sailfish, rooster fish, octopi, squid, and of course feather stars. And that wasn't even close to half of it. I'd rather see a lion fish than a rock star, or a mandarin fish than a famous actor. I know, I'm weird. But it's true.

"Are you doing okay?" Dad asked. When I was younger, he used to try to really win over all my attention before asking a serious question like that. He'd do a simple magic trick, like pulling a coin out of my ear and making it disappear. Then he'd get all serious. But now I'm too old for that. Plus, who needs magic tricks on a whale watch, anyway?

I didn't answer. I pretended his questions got lost in all the chatter on the boat.

"That was amazing," someone behind me said.

"Did you get it?" someone else asked, probably hoping her friend got a picture of the whale. I doubt they got it as well as I did. The trick is to be filming long before you need to. You can delete it later if nothing happens. I wish my shot had been framed better, but it was still cool.

Everyone on this whale-watching boat was getting what they paid for. This humpback was a total show-off.

I didn't put away or even lower the camera on my phone. If a whale surfaced once, it would probably surface again. I knew what I was doing. I pulled my long black hair out of the way and leaned against the railing again. The wind off the Pacific kept blowing it right in front of my phone.

Dad squeezed his paper cocoa cup too tight and now the lid wouldn't fit back on. He just didn't get it. Earlier I'd caught him staring at the floor of the whale-watching boat instead of the ocean.

But I didn't care as long as we weren't having painful conversations. I was here to get some amazing whale documentation and I was doing everything right. Just like I'd been taught. And today it all felt so important. Like the most important thing I'd ever done. Like when a city raises a statue to someone historic. My attitude, my pictures, my love for everything in the ocean was like that kind of statue, but more. I think my heart would crumple if I didn't do it. I had to do this. And love it. And soak it in.

I had to.

I slipped away down the railing and kept scanning the water. Dad didn't follow me. I guess he was either staring at the boat deck again or giving me some space.

It only took half a minute for another spot of ocean to turn from blue to black, and then split as a mound rose out of it. Bingo. This was my football championship. My piano recital. My lead role in the play. This was a live whale right in front of me. And this time I was filming, getting the best footage of my life.

The whale blew water and air out of its huge blowhole. It was like a mini-geyser rocketing out of the ocean. Definitely a humpback. And I bet it was the same one as before.

The whale's mouth looked like a large smile from on top. I love that about humpbacks. And bumps that looked like large warts lined her mouth. I knew they weren't really warts but sometimes, I liked to pretend all humpbacks were just teenagers with acne problems. Really bad acne problems. And somehow, I just knew that this one was a girl whale.

Judging by her size though, she was full-grown, which was cool because female humpbacks grow to be larger than males. Her fins were huge and long. A humpback's fins can be as long as one-third of the length of the whole whale. Its Latin name means "large-winged."

If I was a humpback, I would be able to hold my breath for forty-five minutes and dive 200 meters deep before having to come up for air. I would be able to see the most amazing things. I would be a part of the ocean. And I could swim away from everything if I needed to, or if I just wanted to.

But I wouldn't want to breathe out of the top of my head like a whale. That would just be bizarre.

The crowd clapped and cheered at the humpback, all of them now gathered on the same side of the ship.

I was still filming, just like I should be.

The whale sank back under water.

I didn't put my phone away. A show-stopper like this wasn't done yet. Something was coming. My insides tingled just thinking about it. It was like the humpback knew how important today was. And she was coming through, big time.

It took a little patience. But I was trained to be patient. Trained by the best.

As I waited, tears formed in my eyes and starting streaming down my cheeks. Sometimes they just came. Well, to be honest, they had come lots of times over the past month. Every day. At the worst times. But I wouldn't have them now. I brushed them away. They came again, but I blinked them back. This was the best place in the universe. You don't cry at the water park or at a firework show. No tears on the roller coaster or at the all-you-can-eat buffet. And I definitely wasn't going to cry in the middle of one of my best whale watches ever. Just joy. But I had to be patient. I had to do this right.

And it happened.

While everyone else was talking about the blowhole geyser from a minute ago, the whale shot out of the water right next to the boat. And this wasn't just a little rise. At least twenty feet of her reared out of the water, rotating as she rose. She was like the largest ballerina I'd ever seen. How could something so huge be so graceful? They never caught the majesty of it in all the books, or articles, or even the movies. Not even close.

And then the whale came crashing back down against the ocean, right next to the boat. All 66,000 pounds of her. At least that's the average size of a full-sized female. The landing wasn't nearly as graceful. The ballerina became a linebacker tackling the water. Ka-sploosh! So incredible.

And I filmed it all, waiting to pull my phone in at the last second under the cover of my poncho.

I always wore a poncho on a whale-watching trip. Again, I

was trained by the best. With a poncho, I wouldn't get drenched by all the water the whale splashed up over the whole deck. We'd be swaying and bobbing up and down for minutes after that one. It was like we'd been cannonballed, but by an extra-long bus. Plus, the poncho would protect me if it rained, which it does a lot on our little island off the coast of Washington State.

This was all so cool. Like cooler than the hadal zone, the space in the ocean thousands of feet below water that's basically freezing. Cooler than that.

Not a time for crying. I blinked some more.

"Whoa," someone said, "it soaked us."

"Man, I hope it's not ruined," someone else said, who probably wasn't as fast with their phone as I was. The humpback splashed everything.

"Mine too."

My face was dripping wet, my long black hair clinging to my cheeks and neck where the hood didn't cover. And because this year I'd grown so much, my poncho didn't fit as well as it used to; my legs from the knees down got splashed. But it's okay, because now I'm over five feet tall and can see over some people better than I could before.

I laughed and clapped. Not as loud as I had done it before on other whale watches. I mean, only part of me felt it. But I clapped anyway. I'd seen whales before, but this one was acting like a star at SeaWorld. And she'd splashed us better than if we'd been sitting on the front row.

The whale did its best. Like it knew today was special. I did my best too.

I kept clapping and hooting well after everyone else stopped. But the more I clapped, the more the tears came. It was like they were connected. At least I didn't have to wipe them away. After the humpback drenched us, no one would notice the salty tears mixed in with the ocean water.

I did get quieter when my voice started to break. But I had to cheer. That's what us whale watchers, and dolphin gazers, and sea lion observers do. This was our championship win, our trophy. That was what I was trained to do.

And I was trained by the best.

She really was the best.

I wiped my face again. I wished a wish as big as a blue whale that the best could be here with me. Like she used to be.

CHAPTER 2

In Japan

Willa Twitchell, Journal #2, three years ago

Today I saw French angelfish (<u>Pomacanthus paru</u>) at the aquarium in Seattle with my mom. They aren't in the ocean in Washington, more like Florida or the Bahamas. Yeah, they like it hot. They're beautiful. I love their colors and stripes. They even get married. Well, in a fish kind of way. They don't go on fish dates or anything, but they defend their little spot in the ocean together and eat together. So cute. I've been thinking about them a lot since my parents said they were getting a divorce. I don't get it. They definitely used to love each other more than angelfish do. I don't know what happened.

#IHateDivorce #ICanHashtagMyJournalIfIWant

My mom and dad got a divorce three years ago.

To me, divorce was worse than diving into the water during a shark feeding frenzy. Why couldn't my parents just love each other forever like in the movies?

And if divorce wasn't enough, Mom took a job at the Misaki Marine Biological Station in Tokyo, almost 5,000 miles of ocean away. She was the world expert in feather stars, or crinoids, as the scientists call them. They're beautiful creatures that look like small, colorful ferns. And even though they look like plants, they really are animals, with mouths and everything. You should watch a video of one swimming. They are seriously mesmerizing. The largest ones can reach up to three feet tall, but in fossil form they have been found up to 130 feet long. That's a huge difference. And Misaki paid my mom to study why feather stars don't grow that big now.

My parents gave me the choice: live with Mom or with Dad. Who wants to make a terrible choice like that? Like choosing between ice cream or brownies, or whale watching or tide pools, but an octillion times worse. I was sick for days trying to make the decision. Like in-my-bed-with-a-stomachache sick. Especially because they were going to live so far away from each other. It wasn't like I would be able to visit whoever I wasn't living with on the weekends. But I had to make the choice.

I chose Mom and Japan.

I still get stressed thinking about that decision. I lived in Japan for the last three years, eating all their different foods, seeing their cool sights; like the Tokyo Skytree or DisneySea—it's like Disneyland but with a nautical theme. (Seriously, one of the best ideas in the world.) And I loved the blue whale statue outside the Museum of Nature and Science. I really want to see a real blue whale. They're one of the only whales that swim near both Washington and Japan that I still hadn't seen.

I didn't learn as much Japanese as you'd think. I went to an American school and had friends who spoke English. A lot of them were from other parts of the world, like Ayaan from India, and Guy from England. I spent some time hanging around Mom's work, and when she would go on a research trip I either got to go with her or I was watched by Chihiro, a teacher at my school who was barely out of college. She was nice.

I really missed my dad while I was an ocean away. I even missed his magic tricks. And I didn't get to visit him. At all. Scientists don't get paid a ton and buying a plane ticket back to the US was pricey. Plus, I wasn't a humpback whale that could migrate thousands of miles. I would have if I could.

Instead of visiting, I chatted with my dad every Monday, Wednesday, and Friday for an hour on video call. We tried to talk about life, but Dad and I have never had that much in common. So he learned a few new magic tricks to show me. That was fun for a while, but that fizzled over time too. Pretty soon it was just Monday and Friday.

Then Dad met someone, and we only talked on Mondays.

Her name was Masha—like *Marsha* but without the *r*—and she seemed okay. I talked with her a few times on our Monday chats. I mean, she wasn't nearly as cool as my mom, but she was nice enough.

I didn't go to the wedding. I was invited, and Dad even

offered to fly me out, but I didn't want to be there. It was like Dad was replacing my mom and everyone was going to be happy about it. So I just said it was too expensive.

A year and a half later, the worst thing happened.

The very worst.

I used to think the worst thing that could happen would be being trapped in the Mariana Trench with a zombie worm. They're terrifying. They love to eat bones. You'd think brains, like normal zombies, but nope—bones. Gross. I know.

Okay, they usually only eat bones from fish and whales that are already dead, but it's still creepy.

This was so much worse than being trapped with zombie worms.

A quintillion times worse.

I was in geography class when Mr. Yamamoto checked me out of school. He was a nice old man that worked with my mom, with silver hair and long cheeks, but it was really strange that he checked me out of school. He said we had to hurry to the hospital because my mom had problems with her heart. I knew she took some meds for her heart, but it wasn't anything major. At least, it hadn't been. Inside Mr. Yamamoto's little blue car on the way to the hospital, it felt like something major. It was like all the air around me was thick and serious. Like a giant tsunami wave ten stories tall was about crash onto me and there was nowhere to hide.

By the time we arrived, climbed the hospital steps, and hurried down the hall to room 213, my mother had already passed away.

Gone.

The tsunami hit me. And it destroyed everything.

That's a day I don't think I'll ever stop thinking about.

I stared at Mom in her hospital bed. She looked like a shell of who she had been. Like I was only looking at the sloughed-off exoskeleton. I still have nightmares about it.

And she left me alone in Japan.

CHAPTER 3

Thanking a Humpback

Willa Twitchell, Journal #4, one month ago

Mom is gone.

~~~~~~

After talking on the phone with Grandpa Lowe and my dad, and meeting with Mr. Yamamoto lots of times, Chihiro helped me pack my things and I got on a plane to Seattle. My dad picked me up from the airport and brought me back to Tupkuk Island, the place I had grown up. The place I hadn't been to since I was nine, three years ago.

Dad really tried to help. He hugged me lots. He brought me breakfast in bed when I didn't want to get up. He brought me lunch and dinner, too, on the days I never left my room. He made a few coins disappear and cut a rope and made it whole again. And I'm sure I wasn't a good audience. Once, I even blurted out for him to stop. He wasn't much of a talker, so we didn't say much. Which was fine with me. It was like I was in the blackest part of the ocean and I didn't even know which direction to swim to get out. There were times I cried, and he just rubbed my back.

And now, on the one-month anniversary of my mom's death, I stood on a boat with him. He was worried about me, so he chose something he thought I'd like. Especially something out of the house. It was my first whale watch without her.

And I did like it.

It was just a hard day.

And out on the ocean I saw her everywhere.

I sniffled, then hated myself for doing it. I was so sick of crying. There shouldn't be any crying on a whale watch, unless the whale does something so amazing there are tears of awe. Watching sea creatures was one of my mom's favorite things to do.

I wanted the whale to come back. It seemed like somewhere in her humpback heart she knew I needed her. She had done so well. On some whale watches, you don't see much. That's tragic. Then it's not much of a whale watch; it's just a watch. But for Mom, for today, I needed a little more.

Thankfully, the water bulged up just a little and the humpback surfaced again. It was different though, not a huge, take-my-picture-as-I-shoot-out-of-the-water sort of way. No. She was sneaky like a spy. And she was behind us now and off to one side, coming out just enough for one of her eyes to peer out over the waves. She was probably checking our reactions. Maybe she wanted to see if we loved her show.

I don't think anyone else noticed her. It took a trained eye.

And I had a trained eye.

I snuck through the crowd to the back of the boat, walking slowly up to the rail. I didn't want to spook her. I just looked at that amazing creature and I think she looked back at me. Her eye was bigger than mine, but it worked the same. I mean, I think it was more sensitive to light because it usually looked underwater, but she could see me. Like *really* see me. I could tell, even feel, that she was smart. She wasn't like plankton that just flows with the current. She had thoughts and life and feelings. She was deep and wonderful. And she was looking at me.

Maybe she was on a human watch. Maybe she thought that I was intelligent, too. Maybe she would go home and log everything she remembered in her "humans" journal, just like I did with my ocean journal. No. She didn't have hands, or fingers, and paper wouldn't really work under the water. But maybe she held all that information in her great whale mind.

"Good job, whale," I said, almost whispering to myself. I wanted her to know how much I loved her splashes and back flop. "That was beautiful."

The whale didn't respond.

I wasn't really surprised. I mean, I know whales talk to each other, but they definitely have never spoken with humans. Of course, if they did, it would be a little inconsiderate not to reply when I had just complimented her. Well, at least I think so. I don't know much about whale manners.

The humpback dipped back under the water. If she did understand me, that would maybe even have been a little rude. But I caught a glimpse of movement and followed her around to the far side of the boat, even further away from the crowd. She surfaced again.

"I really needed to see you today," I said. "It's kind of special. I needed to remember . . ." I trailed off.

It almost looked like the whale nodded, like she understood me.

The boat started up again and began to move, churning the water out and moving us forward. But the whale followed.

Maybe she knew I still didn't want her to leave. Whales have amazing instincts. Newborn whales instinctively swim right after they are born. And they know to go to the surface for air, and to go to their mothers for food. Maybe this one knew instinctively that I needed her to stay.

"Thanks," I said as a final word, noticing the whale still approaching the surface.

Then the whale rose again, but this time she came straight up, just barely bobbing her large head above the water. They call it spy hopping. She twisted in the water until she was looking at me with one of her big eyes. And that's when the whale talked back.

CHAPTER 4

Meg

Willa Twitchell, Journal #4, one year ago

Today, while I waited for my mom to get off work, I crouched down in the tide pools outside of the biological station. It was a minus tide, and I could go out further than normal. Inside one of the pockets of rock I spied a long white fuzzy thing moving slowly along the bottom. It had tiny black dots on its "fur" and two pointed ears like a rabbit. But the whole thing wasn't much bigger than my thumb. I looked it up later and people call it a sea bunny even though it's really a slug. The little creature seemed to move with a purpose, though I couldn't guess where it was going. And for a long time I just watched it and wondered what it thought about. I was the only one at that part of the beach, so I talked to it and imagined how it would respond to me. Maybe that's a little crazy, but it seemed like at any moment it would just look up at me (though I never saw eyes on it) and explain what was going on in its little fuzzy brain. Maybe one day we may actually know what animals think.

#IWantToTalkToAnimals #YouKnowYouWantToToo

"Hello, little human," the whale said.

My mouth dropped open so far my tongue practically fell out of my mouth. The whale just spoke back to me.

"Sorry that I didn't respond right away," the whale apologized. "I was kind of . . . well, surprised." I thought a whale's voice would be like garbled thunder, roaring out from under the water—a voice big enough to match its large body. But it wasn't. It was more like an incredible mix of a woman singing with cello playing in the background. Like a one-whale opera. "Not *bad* surprised, like orcas are approaching," she explained, "but *good* surprised, like discovering a pacific snake eel or a hundred-year-old sea turtle." She rolled a little in the water. "Humans have never spoken to me before."

I didn't know if I understood humpback language or if she spoke English, but I knew this was working. And I liked it. Loved it. And something about her sing-songy voice was almost as soothing as the ocean. Maybe it filled a little of my ocean-sized emptiness.

I couldn't believe this was happening. A whale was talking to me. That wasn't even possible, was it? I didn't have time to think or analyze or even doubt. I had to answer back. But it was like trying to talk to a famous scientist. I had loved whales ever since

I was a toddler, but I couldn't go all fangirl and giddy laugh and tippy-toe dance. That wouldn't do. As far as I knew, this was the very first interspecies conversation between human and whale; I had to make a good impression.

I took a deep breath and tried to say something clever. "If it makes you feel any better," I said, "whales haven't ever talked to me either." Not the most insightful thing to say, but hopefully I wasn't embarrassing my species.

The whale nodded, her big snout dipping up, then under the water. Good. That seemed to go over okay.

I was actually talking to a whale. Inside I was full-on screaming in joy. #SoAwesome

"I didn't know that humans ever wanted to talk to us whales," she said, then started to laugh. It sounded like bubbles and an orchestra together. "Usually I come to splash out and give you people a pleasant surprise, not to have a conversation."

"You were absolutely amazing," I said, letting a little of my excitement spill out. "Seriously the best slaps and back flops I've ever seen. And I've been whale watching a lot." I suddenly realized that I was so excited I was speaking in full voice again. I quickly looked around, hoping that no one else had noticed what was going on. I didn't want the crowd to come over and spoil it. So far, I was safe. I think some pelicans were fishing on the other side of the boat and everyone was watching them.

"Oh goodness, I'm not the best out here," the whale said. "I have a friend who can jump so high his tail comes out of the water. His whole family is known for doing leaps together. It's really incredible," she said. "I just want to give you blubberless rectangle-watchers something fun. Even if I know I'm only okay at it."

What had she just said? "Blubberless rectangle-watchers?" I asked.

"Yes," she said. "You're blubberless. You don't have all the attractive fat on you that I have on me. But don't worry, you're still a very cute species."

"Thanks," I said. It wasn't every day a whale called me cute. She had a thick layer of fat all around her to keep her warm in even arctic temperatures. And she was a water-rising, back-flopping acrobat. "What did you mean by rectangle-watchers?" I asked.

"Oh," the whale said, "those little tiny rectangles that most humans look at all the time." She blew a little air out of her blowhole, but she did it quietly. I think she didn't want the crowds to come over either. "All the time," she repeated. "You look at them instead of at each other or at the ocean."

"Rectangles?" I thought hard. "Oh—phones," I said, realizing what she was talking about.

"Is that what they're called?" the whale asked. "They must be hypnotizing, like the bioluminescence of an anglerfish."

I immediately pictured the dot that glows in front of an anglerfish. It is designed to be fascinating, but there are sharp teeth right behind it.

It was strange to think that a whale ever even thought about our phones. "I guess they *are* kind of hypnotizing," I said. "But not like an anglerfish. Not in a dangerous way. I mean, they can also be good. I used one to film you. So I can watch your fantastic jump over and over again."

"You can watch it again?" the whale asked. She bobbed up and down a little in the water.

"Yeah," I said. "Want to see?"

She gave a huge whale nod, then swam in closer to the boat. I leaned my phone over the edge, playing back her latest rise and turn out of the ocean.

When I woke up this morning, I had no idea that I'd be talking to a humpback whale and showing her a video of herself crashing into the ocean. I just thought it was going to be another day of trying not to cry. This was getting better and better.

"Oh, these rectangles are amazing," she said, watching a screen for the first time, "and I didn't do badly at all."

"Not at all," I said.

"Thank you, little human," she said. And I really think she meant it. Again, I wasn't an expert on whale manners, but now that I got to talk to her, she was actually really polite.

My mom would have loved this. Absolutely, nothing held back, loved this. She would definitely fangirl, even if it was just on the inside.

A sting of sadness shot through me. I missed her. But I hated those stings—they were so much worse than stings from a jellyfish. Worse than a stingray jab.

I shook my head. Whale watches are no place for sadness. And whale talks even less.

"My name is Willa," I said, trying to be polite and keep the stings away. "I mean, I guess you could call me 'little human' if you want, but that would mean I would call you 'large whale.'"

The humpback laughed again, like an orchestrated song. "Willa seems like a fine name," she said. "At least as far as humans go. And my name is Megaptera Novaeangliae."

As strange as it sounds, I had heard that name somewhere before. I mean, it's not the name of someone else in one of my classes. That would be some pretty crazy parents if they'd named their human kid Megaptera Novaeangliae. But it was fine for a whale. So where *had* I heard it? I searched my brain files. "That's the scientific name for humpback whales." I felt embarrassed it had taken me so long to realize it.

"You're really bright," the whale said.

I may have blushed a little. I tried really hard to know a lot about marine life, but most people didn't notice or care. "But that can't be your name," I said, thinking this through a little more. "Then every humpback would have the exact same name."

The whale took a moment. "We all share that name."

That seemed strange. "Are you telling me that if you want to shout out to a humpback that is far away you just yell at them, 'Hey, Megaptera Novaeangliae'? Wouldn't they all respond at the same time?"

"What? No!" She laughed more musical bubble sounds. "That's just our name. If I wanted to speak to just one humpback friend, I would use their call."

Oh, so each whale had a specific call. That was pretty much the same as a name. I guess we just didn't understand each other at first. I bet that happened a lot in interspecies friendships. "So we say 'name' and you say 'call.' Let me ask my question differently, then. What is your call?"

"My call is . . ." and she sang a whale song. I tried my best to pay attention to the order of it all. Three sounds like a squeaky balloon, something that sounded a little bit like a Wookie, a door that needs to be greased, and back to the squeaky balloon.

When she stopped, it got quiet.

I wanted to try to say it back, but how was I going to do that? I couldn't make all those sounds, could I? I looked around to make sure that nobody was watching from the boat, then I tried. Three squeaks, a Wookie, creaking door, then another squeak. But they didn't come out right. It sounded more like three pig squeals, a sick tiger, an angry Chihuahua, then another pig squeal. Nothing like the cool sound that the whale just made. I hoped I didn't offend her.

But she didn't get upset. She didn't laugh. At least not out loud. She rolled in the water and I saw her smile. Then again, her mouth always looked like a smile. "That was pretty good," she said. I hoped she wasn't lying. "But you mistakenly called a humpback bull a decent swim away from here. We humpbacks can hear from long distances." She turned and called out in the ocean, listened, then called again. "He thought you wanted to go get some krill with him. I told him that you were a human and probably not looking for a dinner date. That set things straight." She swam a little closer to me. "Unless you *want* to eat krill with him. Do you want me to call him back?"

I shook my head furiously, my cheeks blushing like the scales on a red snapper. I didn't need a whale boyfriend. "I'm sorry. I'm no good at your call," I said. I thought that with some practice I could get it right. But I hadn't really had time to practice. "Maybe I could call you something else until I figure it out. Maybe—" I thought for a moment. "Can I just call you Meg?"

"Meg?" she said.

"Yeah, short for 'Megaptera Novaeangliae.' Sometimes humans shorten names for their friends."

"Oh, I see." I watched her dive down just a little, then resurface.

"Sure," she said. "I like the idea of having a human name and a human friend. It's a pleasant surprise." And she sang it just to prove it. "And I do love pleasant surprises."

I think I'd probably sing more if my song could travel thousands of miles through the ocean like hers.

"When you first spoke to me," Meg said, "you said today was special. That you needed me to appear today. That you needed to remember something. What were you talking about?"

More stings. Lots more.

"Willa," I heard my dad calling, searching for me. That was the last thing I wanted right now. It definitely wasn't every day I got to talk with a live humpback. But he was my dad. He had brought me out here trying to cheer me up. He was trying.

"My dad's calling me," I told Meg. "So I've got to go. I really don't want to, but I have to. Can we talk about this later?" Right after I asked it, I realized I didn't know if there could be a later. "I mean, is there any way I could talk to you again?" I asked. "I would really love it." And I totally meant it.

"I will be around for a while," Meg said, rolling a little onto her back. "And again, I can hear from long distances away. Now that I know your voice, if you just get close to the water and call out, I'll be listening."

That could work? I mean I knew humpbacks could talk to each other when they were hundreds, even thousands of miles apart, but I had no idea one would be listening for me.

I got chills just thinking about how amazing that was. I lived a quick bike ride away from the ocean. Lots of people do when you live on an island.

"You're the best humpback whale ever," I said.

She laughed a song. "That would also be a pleasant surprise," she said.

"Who are you talking to?" my dad asked.

I totally jumped. I knew he was coming, but he still surprised me.

"I was . . ." I turned back out to the ocean, but Meg had swum away. I scanned the rolling water, but couldn't find a trace of her. She must have dived deep and fast. "I was just talking to myself," I said.

He wouldn't have believed me anyway.

CHAPTER 5

Unnoticed

Willa Twitchell, Journal #5,
three and a half weeks ago

The Gulf corvina fish can be the loudest fish in the world. When a few million guy corvinas get together off the coast of California and are all trying to get the attention of all the lady corvinas, they are loud. Like deafening loud. Literally over a million of them gather and researchers have recorded volumes at 150 decibels. That's louder than a jet taking off. It can shake the ships that float by. And it can damage other sea creatures' hearing.

I think my dad's and my stepmom's house is louder than a million corvina fish.

~~~~~~~~~~~~~~~~~~~~~~~~~~~~~

"Get that spatula out of your shirt," my stepmom, Masha, said. "And take it to the sink. I'm going to have to wash it again." She let out an exasperated sigh, staring intently at Caleb, my seven-year-old stepbrother.

"But my back itches," Caleb said, as if what he said was somewhere close to a good reason to have a spatula up his shirt. Caleb was cute, but dumb as a mola mola fish. Thankfully though, he wasn't nearly as huge and awkward. Caleb scratched his back under his Star Wars shirt a few more times with the spatula, his dark eyebrow curling with satisfaction. "It works really good."

"Well," Dad said. "It works *well*."

"See," Caleb said, pointing up at my dad, "Jason thinks it's a good idea." My stepsiblings all called my dad by his first name. That was weird but probably less weird than them calling him Dad.

"I didn't say it was a good idea," Dad said. "I was correcting your grammar." His brown beard moved as he spoke. Masha thinks his beard makes him look handsome. I think it makes him look like a lumberjack or a bristly toadfish.

"I want to try," Nadia said, reaching out for the spatula. She was a few years younger than Caleb and her blonde hair somehow always looked messy even right after she took a shower and brushed it out.

Neither Nadia nor Caleb seemed to care about Dad's grammar lesson.

"Just put the spatula in the sink and sit down for dinner," Masha said, blowing her blonde hair out of her eyes. Her hair looked clean, but by the end of the day it was a little crazy. She had made breaded chicken and homemade fries. It smelled good.

Masha was a better cook than my mom. Maybe the only thing she was better at.

I still didn't really know what to feel about Masha. She was nice to my dad and they seemed okay together. That was good. But she was living in my old house and kissing my dad, which was . . . eww. She was on her phone a lot, which was annoying since she had kids to take care of. A lot of kids. She was pretty much a guppy. Guppies can give birth to as many as two hundred babies at a time. Masha didn't give birth to them all at once, and she didn't give birth to two hundred, but four kids was a lot. She brought the older three with her when she married my dad two years ago. And then had another one. They all seemed like their volume dials were turned up way too high. It was like they had to talk over each other to ever be heard. So in general, I just don't say anything and retreat to my room whenever I can.

And that's strange. Usually I'm a talker.

Years ago, in this same house, it was just my mom, my dad, and me. Three people. We talked a lot, but not constantly. I used to be able to hear the refrigerator hum while I was working on my homework. Or the crickets at night. But now we had seven people in our house. We more than doubled. And I had to share space with Masha, Caleb, Nadia, Garth, and baby Hannah. Hannah was only one year old, cuter than a mandarin fish, and louder than a barking sea lion.

I wanted my mom back more than ever. She never shouted. She just wasn't that type. Masha shouted every day. Things like, "Dinner!" or "Brush your teeth!" or "Get that spatula out of your shirt!" And there was something about seeing Masha that made me miss my mom more. It was like she was a reminder of what I used to have.

Things were different with my dad too. When it was just mom and him, they both worked, so neither one of them had to work crazy hours. But now that it's just him (Masha doesn't work) and a million people in this house to take care of, he's gone all of the time. He's an accountant for the city but takes late-night jobs doing other people's taxes and doing books for some companies. I mean, he's still around, but I miss him. And he's just different. Quieter. Less fun. No magic tricks. I don't know if it's because of problems I don't know about or what, but he's not the same guy I left here three years ago. I don't think it's Masha's fault—he smiles when he sees her—but I can't put my finger on what it could be.

"Open up," Masha said, trying to get Garth to eat his chicken.

He shook his head. "It's gross," he said. His voice would have been adorable if he didn't talk like he thought we were on the other side of the island. How could anyone be so adorable and completely annoying at the same time?

"Is not," Nadia said, a little louder than Garth. As if we needed anything louder.

"Is too," Garth said, even louder. I think he was trying to win the argument by blowing out our eardrums.

"Not!" Nadia screamed.

"Quiet," Masha called out, louder than them all. "You two have been fighting all day and I'm done with it."

Definitely not like my mom.

The table went quiet.

Like the eye of a storm.

"We saw a humpback whale yesterday," I said, trying to change the tone of the meal. And trying to get back to my talkative self.

"What's a humpback?" Caleb asked. Again, dumb as a mola mola fish.

I tried not to show my annoyance at having to explain what a humpback whale is to a seven-year-old. I mean, who trained this kid? "It's one of the coolest creatures in the world," I said. "It was bigger than a bus and weighed tons and tons. If it landed on this house it could squash us all flat. Here, I got some video. Let me show you," I started to reach for my phone. It wouldn't be as cool as showing it to Meg, but they should still be impressed.

"Was that on the special boat ride Jason took you on because your mom died?" Nadia asked with a smile. A huge, cornbread-in-her-mouth-but-she-just-couldn't-keep-from-talking smile.

I froze. Stings. A septillion of them.

I'm sure Nadia didn't mean to send them, but she did. Masha or my dad must have told her about it.

"Yes," my dad said, and then couldn't seem to say anything else.

I couldn't get over Nadia's gigantic smile. Everything inside me felt like the opposite of a smile, but there she was just beaming. She wasn't sad about my mom. She didn't even know her. I looked at everyone at the table. None of them except my dad even knew her. None of them were sad. And my dad had divorced her. He let her leave to the other side of the world. And he didn't visit us once in Japan. There was no way he missed her like I did. I was the only one trapped in this bloom of jellyfish. The stings, like harpoons, jabbed me all over.

"I'm sorry," Masha said, apologizing to me for Nadia. "And we're really sorry about . . ." Just then Hannah reached for Nadia's drink and sent apple juice splashing all over the table. "Oh, Hannah!" Masha nearly screamed. She grabbed her youngest daughter out of her chair before she could get drenched in dripping juice. Dad got up and rushed for some towels. Caleb laughed and Nadia told him it wasn't funny.

I couldn't take it. And I wasn't hungry anymore. I slipped out of my chair, put my dish in the sink, and in all of the confusion, slid out the front door.

I didn't tell them any more about Meg. They were worried about the spill.

And they would probably never remember to ask about my video. My spectacular video.

My mom would have wanted to know all about it.

I was supposed to ask before I left the house, but I hadn't done that in a while. Almost every day this week I'd snuck out after dinner. Well, I actually wasn't that sneaky. Just nobody was watching. They probably assumed I was doing homework or looking at my ocean books in my room.

And with all the loud kids and loud Masha, no one noticed.

Or they didn't care.

CHAPTER 6

Risky

Willa Twitchell, Journal #5,
a week and a half ago

Lots of fish and sea creatures live in large groups called pods. Some of these pods are huge. A cruise-ship captain once saw a dolphin pod that he estimated had 100,000 dolphins in it. 100,000! I wish I could have seen that. Fish can swim in pods of so many that nobody could possibly count them all.

But then there are rabbitfish. They don't look like rabbits at all. Well, I guess their mouths kind of look like rabbit mouths, but that's it. The most common type are mostly yellow with a black-and-white-striped face. They don't usually live in huge pods or schools. They just have one really good friend. They look for food together and explore the ocean as a team. Just two.

I'm more of a rabbitfish than a dolphin. And Marc Antonio Mendoza used to be my buddy rabbitfish. We were inseparable when we were younger. I cried and cried when I had to say goodbye to him to go to Japan. We texted a little for a while, but I hadn't talked to him for almost a year when I came back to the island and saw him again. I was pretty nervous. He was older now, and I was too, but he had made other friends while I was gone. I'm not sure he needs me anymore. I've only been to school a week and a half and have talked with him a few times, but our conversations were awkward. I'm not sure if he even wants to be friends again.

~~~~~~

I tossed my phone between my hands before I got up the courage to do something risky. Something that made my palms slimy like eel skin.

I texted Marc. I still had his number.

I don't know why I did it. Maybe all the stings were getting to me and I needed a friend.

One time I texted my mom, complaining about Kimi, this spoiled girl in my science class in Japan. She invited me to her party, but I didn't want to go. She was really annoying. And my mom texted back,

> It wouldn't hurt you to go.
> Everyone needs friends.

At first, I thought she was talking about Kimi, and I think she was, but then I realized she was also talking about me.

I needed more friends.

I've read that text about three thousand times. I read all my mom's texts over and over. My mom would want me to get friends. Maybe that was part of why I texted Marc too.

Okay. There was no maybe about it.

So I took a deep breath and pressed the little arrow to send the text.

As soon as it was sent, I reread it to make sure that it didn't sound too needy. Why did I always do that? It would be so much more helpful to reread it when I could actually change it.

> Hey, Marc! Want to meet me at the tide pools? Just like old times. I have to get out of the house and it's a low tide so there should be good stuff. I'm heading there now.

Not too embarrassing.

Marc and I first started hanging out in the third grade. When he was new, our teacher, Mrs. Loose, assigned me to show him around. He was really nice and funny and after a couple of recesses, that was it. We'd been hanging out ever since. We did a project in fourth grade together where we had to make puppets of important historical figures and tell their story. I picked Jacques Cousteau. He was a French explorer who practically invented scuba diving and then filmed a bunch of awesome creatures in the ocean and showed them to the world. He also stopped people from dumping waste in the ocean. Seriously amazing guy. Marc chose the guy who invented Mario and Donkey Kong at

Nintendo—Shigiru Miyamoto. Not as cool as Jacques Cousteau, but still cool. Marc's a bit of a video-game fanatic.

Later that year, Marc and I took second place in the school science fair. We did an experiment to see if fish change their breathing, and even change their color as you raise the temperature.

And then I left.

When I came back a few weeks ago, I hoped everything would just go back to the way it was when we were nine. But Marc was taller and different. He used to be super cheerful and easygoing, but now he wasn't as much. He was . . . different. He still smiled a lot, but sometimes he seemed thoughtful, and sometimes he maybe even looked like a black musselcracker, which I think are the grumpiest and angriest-looking fish in the ocean. He ate lunch with Luke and Nash and played video games with them after school. It wasn't like he was trying to ignore me or be mean to me. Maybe he just didn't know where to fit me back into his life. Or maybe he was trying to figure out if I even fit.

I hoped I fit. I hoped he would answer my text.

I dropped my phone in my pocket and grabbed my bike from the shed. My mountain bike was as blue as the ocean and a couple sizes below adult. I was probably getting too big for it, but it was still great to get it back.

Zipping down the street, I was like a sailfish shooting through the water. They can swim almost seventy miles per hour and are probably the fastest fish in the ocean.

I was that fast.

Okay. Not seventy miles per hour, but for a twelve-year-old girl riding a bike, I wasn't bad. My black hair floated in the air behind me, and if I happened to cry, not that I was doing *that* again, I was going fast enough that the wind would whip the tears right off my face.

That's right. I was at tear-whipping speed.

But I didn't feel like crying right now. No stings. I was too nervous about the text I just sent to Marc. What was he thinking right now? That I was a total weirdo? Capital-*W* Weirdo? Or maybe he kind of liked that I texted him. My mind alternated between the options and everything in between.

I almost felt bad because I didn't have stings. Like maybe I should have them all the time.

But I kept pedaling.

My family's house stood on a couple acres and the closest neighbor owned a horse ranch, so I rode my bike a lot. There were little community neighborhoods closer to town, but I was glad I didn't live there. I'd be further from the ocean, and the kids in my class from over there had more money and were more stuck up. Except Marc, of course. Even though his family always had money, he was really nice.

Hopefully he was still as nice as I remembered him.

No matter how many times I had ridden this path in the past, the uneven, hard-packed dirt always had surprise bumps and dips, so I had to stand on my pedals to absorb the shock. Something about pushing forward felt good.

Once the trees cleared, I reached the highway that stretched along the coastline. I'm always extra careful when crossing the highway. One time when I was seven, I saw a car just blow down the road and totally run over an otter that was crossing to the inlets. I don't want to ever be that poor otter.

I skidded to a stop on the other side of the highway and parked my bike next to a tree. I could see the ocean and hear it crash, but I still had to shimmy down a natural rock wall before getting there. There was a tricky and thin, crooked trail with a couple of difficult parts that I could take but almost never did. Climbing down the rocks was faster.

I loved that this beach was hard to get to. It kept other people away. Out of sight, out of mind. It was like my very own beach.

Down in less than a minute, I ran up to the ocean, standing right in front of the breaking waves. There wasn't much wind, which was unusual for Washington. The quiet made the ocean sound even more powerful.

In and out.

Like the ocean was breathing.

I was always careful around it; it was a force to be reckoned with. The ocean could crush whole cities in a tsunami. And yet it was also peaceful. Something about the deep sound and its repetition entranced me.

Once in music class, we did this experiment where we hit a tuning fork and it vibrated and made a cool sound. Then all we had to do was put another tuning fork next to it and it vibrated too. We didn't even have to hit it. It recognized the sound waves and resonated with the first tuning fork. They affected each other. They sang the same song.

That was the ocean and me.

It sings my soul song. #Connected

I breathe with it. And I think with it. And my heart matches the rhythm.

Okay. Maybe that's a little much, but that's what it feels like. And it was the best thing about living here.

Masha and her kids didn't feel it. I mean, since I'd been home, they hadn't gone to the ocean once. That's *weeks*. Which is hard to do when you live on an island. It was probably just a huge swimming pool to them.

My phone buzzed. With that one sound, I lost all the calm the ocean brought. Was that Marc? What had he texted back?

> K

Not much of an answer, but I think a hundred minnows swam through me, sending little bits of happiness all over. He said okay. Maybe I had worried too much about this. Maybe he wanted to pick it up where we left off too.

Another text from Marc:

> If you do a favor for me.

A favor? So this was a trade? Some of the minnows swam away. That didn't sound as much like best friends. He would only hang out with me if I did something for him. It was more like business partners and I was basically going to pay for his time.

But friends ask for favors too, right? Maybe I was reading too much into this.

What would he ask for? Maybe borrow some money? No. His dad owned the Mendoza Marina. They fixed and docked almost everybody's boats on the island and some from the other islands, and some from all over the world: small fishing boats to million-dollar yachts. Plus, I think his mom did investment stuff from home. It wasn't like they were millionaires, but they did really well.

Maybe Marc needed me to ask my dad to give him a ride somewhere? But that wouldn't make sense. Both Marc's parents could drive, plus we could ride our bikes most places on the island.

Maybe he wanted me to find out if some girl liked him? That was the most probable. In fact, that would be something I could do better than Luke or Nash. Then again, I wasn't really friends with any girls, especially since I'd just been back on the island for a few weeks, and back at school for only a week and a half.

Or maybe he just wanted me to lend him our Xbox. His little brother had spilled lemonade on his and fried it. At least that's what Marc had posted on Instagram.

> Favor?

I texted.

Then I tried to think of something clever. I needed my friend back and he liked clever.

> I saw your sad Xbox on Insta. I can't lend you ours. My stepsibs would kill me. #LikeSeriouslyKillMe 😵

> Lol. That's not it.

Lol. That was good. And it felt great to text back and forth a little. We had done that a few times when I lived in Japan. I took a bunch of pictures of Miyamoto's childhood home and the Nintendo headquarters when we visited Kyoto and sent them to Marc. He liked that. But the time difference always made that tricky and most of our conversations fizzled after just a couple texts.

I waited for Marc to tell me the favor.

And I waited more. What was that about? Did he want me to guess?

> I'll tell you when I get there.

He finally texted.

> See you in 10.

Okay. This was good, right?

CHAPTER 7

400 Blue Whales Away

Willa Twitchell, Journal #2, three years ago

Today we went to the aquarium for school. It's funny that they put us on a bus to go see ocean animals when we live right on the ocean.

But I loved the walrus tank. They only had two walruses and one was sleeping most of the time. The other one was playing with visitors at the glass. He would put his flipper where your hand was. He would get out of the water and then dive in, smashing his squishy face into the glass. He seemed to be having so much fun and I just wanted to get to know him better. You know, find out what his walrus mind was thinking.

#AndIWasKindOfJealousOfHisAwesomeTusks

Marc had texted that he would be there in ten minutes, but I doubted it. He was usually really good at being on time, but he couldn't bike that fast from his place. Not possible. More like fifteen if he was really fast. So that should give me a little more time to talk to Meg while I waited.

That was, if I could actually talk to Meg again.

I looked down the shore to my left and right. No one in sight.

I don't know why I looked; no one came here. It was too steep to come down. Everyone else picked easier access beaches with sand. #Weaklings

Well, there *was* Jean Lambert, the old lady who lived closest to this beach on the north end. Her property backed this beach and she was still limber enough to shimmy down the steep trail. She always wore a crazy bucket hat—basically just a hat with a floppy rim that went all the way around it. Jean had lots of different colors of bucket hats, but they were always the same style. She used to talk with me and Mom for a long time. She asked lots of questions. The curious type.

I hope when I get old, I still ask a lot of questions.

"Meg," I called out.

No answer. I stepped closer to the water before trying again. Humpbacks can hear for thousands of miles, but maybe I had to be closer to the ocean for my voice to carry. Or maybe I had to put my face actually in the water. No—it worked last time when I was just close. Maybe she couldn't recognize my voice. We had been far from the west shore when I met her after all, a totally different place. And it had been a whole day.

I tried one more time, calling out her name.

Silence again.

I thought about using her call. What was it? A few squeaks, then a Wookie noise, then . . . wait. I didn't want to ask a male humpback out to dinner again. With my luck I'd mess up and ask him to marry me. #IReallyDontWantToMarryAWhale

"Wiiiilllllllllaaaa," I finally heard back. She sang my name like it was an anthem or something. Like she was introducing me at a concert in some huge auditorium. "My favorite little human."

It made me feel like a rock star.

Maybe everyone should have a whale to talk to. They can make a person feel pretty special.

"I'm so glad you can hear me," I said.

"Oh, I hear you loud and clear," she sang-said.

"Where are you?" I asked, looking out over the waves, hoping she would jump out and give me another back flop.

"I'm just out looking for some more plankton," Meg said. "I love plankton. But a little mackerel would be even better." She sang the word *mackerel* more than the others. "But I don't think I'm too far from you. Probably about four or five hundred blue whales or so."

"Four *hundred* blue whales?" I asked, immediately imagining a giant group of the largest animals in the world. "Wait. You are using them to measure distance, right?"

"Of course," she said. "How do you measure distance? We use the largest animal there is to tell you how far away we are." I guess that made sense. "I could measure in dolphins if you'd like, but the numbers get pretty big."

"No thanks," I said, doing the calculations in my head. Blue whales were the largest animals on earth and could get to be one hundred feet long. That's longer than a basketball court. Can you imagine something swimming by that was the size of a basketball court? Incredible. 400 blue whales in a row, nose to tail, had to be several miles. I didn't want to figure that out right now. I'm a marine biologist, not a mathematician.

"I can only talk for a few minutes," I said. "My friend is coming, and I don't know if he'd understand that I was talking to a whale. Especially a whale 400 blue whales away." I could only imagine his reaction. He would probably do that crazy crooked smile that looks forced. Hopefully he wouldn't make the grumpy musselcracker face.

"Oh, I love friends," Meg said. "And I get it. I don't think my pod would understand that I'm talking to a human."

That made me laugh a little. It was crazy that we could talk to each other. Crazy and wonderful.

"So tell me about your friend," Meg said.

"Um," I started, wondering where to begin, "his name is Marc. He used to be my best friend, but I moved away and then back and now—"

"Like a migration?" Meg interrupted.

I thought about it for a moment. "Yeah, I guess so," I said and splashed the water caught between the pebbles on the beach with the bottom of my shoes. "I left with my mom and lived in Japan for a while, but . . ." I got to the part of the story about my mom and stopped. The words clumped up inside my throat. I couldn't talk about her dying right now. I had just met Meg the other day and we only had a few minutes before Marc came. Plus,

I was trying not to think about it. About her. I didn't want Marc to show up and find me all red-eyed and puffy from crying. "But . . . then I came back," I said.

"Are you okay?" Meg asked. "You sounded like something caught in your throat. Like, once a friend of mine got a mouthful of fish near the surface, and caught a pelican in there too. Yuck."

I didn't think missing my mom had anything to do with an unwanted pelican in a whale's throat, but I liked that she worried enough to ask. "I'm fine."

"Good," Meg said. "It's so great to see a friend after a long migration. Are you excited?"

"Yeah," I said, "but also really nervous. I think he might have changed a lot."

"Oh, I know that feeling," Meg said. "A lot can change after a migration."

"Definitely," I said. "I'm not even sure he still thinks we're friends."

Meg didn't even hesitate. "Don't worry," she said. "He'll definitely still want to be your friend. I barely know you and am super excited to be your friend." There it was again. She made me feel so good. Everyone should have a whale to talk to. "But," Meg continued, "you said it was a 'he-friend,' like a male human?"

"Yeah," I said.

"Ooooooooooooh," she held out the musical sound so long it almost sounded like a call. "So do you lipsmack him?"

"Lipsmack?" I shook my head. "What are you talking about?"

"That strange thing you humans do," Meg explained. "I often

see you on boats. You put your fins around each other and lips-mack, right on the mouth."

Kissing? I was being asked about kissing from a whale?

"No," I said emphatically. And that was true. "It's called kissing. And I don't kiss Marc. I haven't even thought about it."

"Okay," Meg said. "I was just curious. Plus, if you did, that bull humpback you asked for a dinner date yesterday would probably be jealous." Her laugh rumbled a little through the water.

"Let's change the subject," I said. My cheeks were getting hot, like a hypothermal vent on the ocean floor. I really didn't want to talk about kissing.

"Oh, I've got one," Meg said. "You were going to tell me something on the boat before you had to meet your dad. Something about you needing to remember something . . ."

I had been remembering the best. Remembering my mom.

I didn't want to talk about her. But I also really *did* want to talk about her. It was strange—like talking about her would be a long treacherous swim, but I knew at the end there could be a cool, beautiful coral reef. But the treacherous swim was terrifying.

My hands shook a little and my pulse raced, but I managed to start, "I've had a really hard time lately . . ."

Footsteps ran up behind me. "Hey, Willa." The voice was higher than most twelve-year-old boys.

Marc. He was here. Terrible timing, though. And early. It was close to ten minutes, just like he said. How did he get here so fast?

"Well," Meg said, "go on." I don't think she heard Marc. Maybe he wasn't close enough to the water yet.

I didn't go on. I couldn't just keep talking to Meg, who Marc couldn't even see. Plus, she was a whale. I'd seem like an absolute crazy person, a marine biologist gone insane. Then again, if I hadn't actually talked with a whale myself, I don't know if I'd believe it. Maybe I really *was* an absolute crazy person. Nothing like coming back to a school after three years and giving people that impression.

"Who were you talking to?" Marc asked, flipping his head to get his long dark bangs out of his eyes. He didn't seem weirded out or anything. Apparently, he couldn't hear Meg, like she couldn't hear him. Or at least he didn't understand her.

I smiled, trying to look innocent. I had no idea what to say. It wasn't like I was going to tell him the truth.

During my silence, Meg called out again, "Willa? Are you there?"

I looked sideways at Marc. "Did you hear that?"

Marc tilted his head. "The ocean?"

So he didn't hear it, not even whale noises. I wasn't sure if I was relieved or sad. "Yeah, the ocean. Beautiful, isn't it?"

He looked confused but nodded.

"Is *Marc* there?" Meg asked. "You're not lip smacking, are you?"

Really?

Maybe everyone *doesn't* need their own whale.

CHAPTER 8

Marc

Willa Twitchell, Journal #5, Today

Some of my favorite places in the world are the tide pools. Especially my tide pools. Before I was old enough to snorkel or even walk, my mom took me there. I don't remember it, but I've seen pictures of her pointing things out to chubby-baby me.

I love the rock formations that the waves cover during high tide, but don't quite reach during the low. They let a bunch of critters and plants into holes in the rocks at high tide and then leave them stranded there in the low. That means at the right time, those pools get filled with ocean life trapped until the tide rises again. It's like a little temporary ocean zoo. My little zoo.

"I'm just excited to see the tide pools," I finally said, trying to cover up the fact that I was talking to a whale several miles away about not kissing Marc. So embarrassing.

But it wasn't a total lie. I *was* really excited. This was the first low tide I had made it down to the beach. And a minus tide meant that we would find extra stuff. And Marc was here.

He grinned and shook his head. "You're so weird."

"Yeah," I admitted, willing my face not to look like red algae, "but I'm the fun kind of weird, right?" I really hoped I was. I mean, I knew I was unique. I was probably the only girl at our middle school who geeked out about tide pooling. But I didn't want Marc to hang out with me just as some sort of charity work for an old friend.

Marc shrugged, like he wasn't sure what kind of weird I was. My insides dropped like a boulder into the ocean.

But then Marc playfully pushed me on the shoulder. He was just kidding. That made it better. At least I think it did. I hoped he meant that of course I was the fun kind of weird and this was like old times, like we were in third or fourth grade again. I hoped it didn't mean that he was just teasing me because I really was the weird kind of weird.

We started walking toward the rocks and puddles of the tide pools. "So, did you hear a whale call a few seconds ago?" I asked. I knew he said he didn't hear anything, but I wanted to be sure.

He shook his head.

Maybe this was some sort of special ability I had or had trained my ears to hear. But I didn't ask any more; I didn't want to sound crazy.

When we got to the tide pools, we had to step carefully. There were two reasons for that: One, many tiny plants and animals cling to the rocks. If you walk softly and carefully you can keep from crushing them. And two, these tide pool rocks are vicious sharp. They can cut up your feet and leave them looking like you tangled with an angry blue crab, so we always wear shoes when tide pooling. Flip-flops aren't enough.

"Hey, check it out," I said, squatting down over a puddle in the rocks and pointing. Scuttling around a mossy leaf was a tiny pink crab. "A baby Dungeness." I dug my phone out of my pocket and took a few pictures.

"Cool." Marc slowly crouched beside me. He used to be a lot faster. I didn't know if he was slow because he was only pretending to be interested, or if he was tired, or maybe just playing it cool. Then he talked to the crab. "One day you will grow big and strong."

I almost couldn't believe it. I talked to whales and Marc talked to crabs; it's like we were connecting again.

"And," Marc added, still talking to the crab, "when you are big enough, you will become my dinner."

Well, that wasn't the same type of thing at all.

I slapped Marc on the arm. "That's mean," I said.

"What?" Marc said. "I was just giving her a goal, a dream to aspire to."

I rolled my eyes and opened my backpack. Marc had grown and changed since I was gone. And the joke was still kind of his style, but different. I took out a big ziplock bag. Inside was my ocean journal. Well, it was my fifth one. My mom kept journals.

She logged everything she saw, put the date, the time, the location, even the weather. And then after, she sometimes wrote down what was happening in her life. She said that a good scientist had to be a good observer, even about themselves. She said we could learn from watching creatures and from noticing things about our own lives. So I'd been doing the same thing for a long time. I flipped to an open page and wrote down about seeing the Dungeness. I would print out at least one of the pictures I had taken later and glue it in. Or I'd sketch one in.

Maybe I'd write about meeting up with Marc, too. I hoped it would be a good entry.

"Still doing the journal thing?" he asked.

I looked up and waved the book around. "I think the answer is pretty obvious." I was trying to act confident, but it came off a little smart-mouthed. I guess my jokes had changed as well.

His eyes returned to the Dungeness. "Do you think she gets scared in there, waiting for the tide to rise up again? I mean, she made a pretty terrible choice and now she probably feels totally stuck."

"What terrible choice?" I asked, still scratching a few notes in my journal.

"She swam too close to shore and got caught in a trap," he said, gesturing toward the small pool of water.

"Maybe she swam here to escape something big chasing her," I said. "This could be a sanctuary." Marc gave me an I-hadn't-thought-about-that face. "Plus, she'll be fine," I said. "She could climb out if she really needed to. And, unless she flips over, we don't even know if it *is* a she. Just because it's pink doesn't make it a girl."

Marc raised his hands. "Sorry, I was just guessing. It would taste good either way."

I sighed and watched the little crab scurry across the puddle floor.

We watched for a little while longer. I thought I'd give Marc a chance to ask about his favor, but he didn't seem to want to take it. So I started up again. "Do you still want to help the world take down all the killer zombies?" I asked.

He looked at me and smiled. "Some things never change."

Marc's always wanted to design video games. And a game full of zombies was one of his ideas years ago. It was pretty cliché. At least he thought of interesting locations, like taking down zombies in the Amazon, on a cruise ship, and in Yellowstone National Park. That helped a little. He said you'd be able to push a zombie into the Old Faithful geyser.

"But I've got some better ideas, too," Marc said. "Just had one. Just now." He tapped the side of his head. "What if I made a game where you got shrunk and you had to make your way through the tide pools? And the crabs were hungry? And the other creatures tried to get you?"

"That's actually a good idea." I said. "I would probably even play that one."

"Whoa," he said, tilting his head so his floppy hair moved out of his eyes. "You've never said that before."

"You never had a game idea about the ocean before," I said.

This wasn't going bad at all. The more we hung out, the more it felt like old times.

We both moved to the next pool and crouched down. I gave him another minute to ask his favor, but again, he didn't. He used to be a lot more talkative. Maybe it wasn't as much like old times. "Speaking of things that didn't happen before," I said. "I don't think you ever rode to the beach as fast as you did today." Just saying that made me feel good. When it had happened, I was so distracted by Meg that I didn't realize how cool it might be. It was like he really wanted to hang out with me.

"Well, I . . ." he faltered for a second. Was he embarrassed that he got here so quickly? Like maybe he was excited and he didn't want to admit it? "I was just coming from the marina. It isn't that far away."

That made sense, and not as cool as if he was excited to hang out. His dad's marina was a lot closer to the tide pools than his house.

But he had come fast. That was good.

While we looked at a bunch of barnacles in one of the pools, I wished everything was like before and I could talk about anything. I kind of wanted to talk about my mom eventually. Not now. That would be too fast. What would I say? "It's good to hang out again. Did you hear that my mom died?" So awkward. Maybe I wished I was like a barreleye fish and he could just see it on my mind. Barreleye fish are awesome that way. They have this transparent bubble over their heads and you can see right in. It's like you can see the pilot in a cockpit. You can really only see their eyes in there, but it seems like you can see their mind.

Then again, I wasn't sure he was the talk-about-hard-stuff kind of friend anymore. He wasn't even looking at the tide pool, just staring out into the ocean. And his crooked smile was fighting with his grumpy musselcracker face. It worried me a little. I tapped his knee with the back of my hand. "Are you okay?"

He looked back at me and nodded. "Sorry, just thinking about . . . stuff."

I waited and he didn't say anything else. I really hoped he wasn't thinking about how to tell me that I'm awkward and weird and how the ocean obsession and looking at tide pools was fun as kids, but not anymore.

CHAPTER 9

Almost

Willa Twitchell, Journal #3, two years ago

I was watching sea otters with my mom today and realized that Marc was basically just a human version of an otter. They have dense fur (he has thick hair), usually eat 25% of their body weight every day (easily), and they belong in the water (Marc could swim all day). Oh yeah, and they keep their snacks under their armpits for safekeeping.

#LOL #MyFriendIsASeaOtter

A small wave moved the water from one pool to the next. "Did you know there are waterfalls under the ocean?" I asked Marc, brushing aside a large piece of seaweed.

"What?" Marc said. "That doesn't even make sense."

"Yes, it does," I said, standing up to stretch after all of that crouching. "It's where warm water and cold water meet. One is forced under and it becomes a waterfall under the ocean. There are rivers and stuff too."

Why was I talking about underwater waterfalls? Was I trying to impress him? Like wow him back into being my friend? I needed to stop being so nervous. I was making things weird.

"That's cool," Marc said. He said that a lot. Well, he used to. Maybe some things don't change much. "I'm going to look that up on YouTube. Just to make sure you aren't a liar."

"No, you won't," I said, calling his bluff. I thought some teasing might be good. Things had gotten weird there for a minute. "You'll forget about it."

He laughed. That was good.

My mind wandered back to the favor. It couldn't be something like "go to the dance together," could it? They'd announced that there would be one at the end of May and I hadn't been at this middle school long enough to know how people did dances on the island. In Japan, we all just went like it was a party. Maybe that's what they do here and he wants me to go with him so he can have a friend. After all, Marc was the kid who would drag me all around because he never liked to go anywhere by himself. Not the store. Not the snack bar line. Not the bathroom. (Don't worry—I waited outside.)

"Willa? Marc? Are you two back on my beach?" a worn voice asked. I hadn't heard it in years. I looked up to see Jean Lambert making her way across the tide pool towards us, when we all spotted something red pop out of a puddle and slither across the rock into another puddle. Jean stopped and pointed. "Did you see that octopus?" We made our way over to check it out.

I hadn't talked with Jean since I got back. I mean, I saw her once from a ways away. To be honest, I kind of hid so she wouldn't speak to me. I just didn't want to talk to her then. I guess I was getting pickier about who I talked to and when. Nothing against Jean. She was really nice. I just didn't want to talk.

"Is this one of the kinds where the males have the babies?" Marc asked as we walked toward Jean.

I stopped and looked at him sideways. "Do you mean a seahorse?"

"No, that special kind of octopus," Marc said without pausing. "Or am I mixing them up?"

I caught up with him. "You're definitely mixing them up. Male seahorses carry the babies and octopi die a little while after they have their babies."

"That's intense," he said as we continued to a shallow puddle with a partially covered red octopus. It was about ten inches long.

"I think it's a Giant Pacific," Jean said. "But it's not too giant yet."

They were known for scrounging around the tide pools for a small crab snack every once in a while. Judging by its size it was really young. They can get up to like sixteen feet.

Before we could crouch down, Jean hugged us both. She had never done that before. It wasn't that I didn't like it, I just didn't expect it. "It's so good to see you two," she said. "Both of you back here." I couldn't help but smile. "It's almost like before."

Almost.

I hated that word. I knew why it wasn't just like before. Someone was missing.

A million jellyfish stings again.

I had been so worried about what Marc's favor would be and hoping we'd be friends again, I had forgotten about my mom for a few minutes. And then my next thought was how wonderful it had been to forget for even just a little while.

More stings.

Guilty stings. How could I have forgotten?

"I was so sorry to hear," Jean said, and then her voice cracked a little, "about your mom." She hugged me again.

A whirlpool of anger, depression, and a bit of happiness swirled together inside me. Anger and depression for the same reason: Mom was gone. It suddenly took everything in me to not collapse in a mound of weeping girl. But there was a little happy too. Happy because Jean remembered her. And she loved her enough to get choked up about her when she spoke. She loved Mom too. They were friends, even though Jean was old enough to be Mom's mother.

I didn't know what to say, especially with the twisting and churning inside me. I tried to push against the sting, just enough to smile and nod. Thankfully Marc crouched down, looked at the little octopus and spoke. "Whoa. That's crazy." The octopus moved in a slimy mess out of the puddle and toward another. Its slither-walking was eerie and awesome. Then it slipped into a corner, covering itself with splotchy white dots.

"Oooh, and look at it camouflage," Jean said, pointing.

That fantastic octopus changed the subject for me. I loved

it so much. "Did you know that the octopus has three hearts?" I asked, trying to keep the focus on the creature.

"Is Willa making that up?" Marc asked Jean. Why would he trust Jean over me? I probably knew more than she did.

She shook her short white curls. "It's true," she agreed. "And Marc, I heard you moved," she said.

"Yeah," he said, then he turned to get a better view of the octopus.

"Are you liking it?" she asked.

Marc gave a nod without looking at either of us. I hadn't known that. Obviously we had some catching up to do.

"Well, I won't keep you forever," Jean said. "I could talk your ears off if left to it." She was kind of right. "Go on. Have some fun. It was good seeing you." She waved us off, so we started back to another spot in the tide pools. Secretly, I was grateful she cut off the conversation. I didn't think Marc was going to ask for his favor in front of her.

As we moved over the next few puddles, life felt closer to right than it had in a long time. I was at the tide pools with Marc and Jean. It was like a piece of me was back. "So . . ." I said, deciding to be forward again. "Are you ready to tell me what this favor is?"

Marc looked back at me, giving away only a little corner of a smile. But it wasn't mischievous, or sad. It was . . . different.

He opened his mouth, then closed it again.

"Never mind," he said, shaking his head. "Thanks for inviting me down." And then he turned and started walking away from the beach, back toward his bike.

"Wait," I said, "are you sure?" This was why he came, after all.

"Yeah," he said. "Forget it." He waved me off while still walking away.

And I knew I wouldn't. I couldn't forget it. And it made me feel like I wasn't enough of a friend or business partner or whatever to even ask.

CHAPTER 10

Skipping Rocks for It

Willa Twitchell, Journal #5, today

I didn't see that coming.

My palms got slimy like eel skins again. I knew what I needed to say, but it was scary.

A lot of me really wanted to just let Marc walk back to his bike and go. But I just couldn't. There was something about not having a friend right now that threatened to sink me.

I ran and caught up.

"Hey," I said, "c'mon. You said you would only come here if I did a favor for you. You might as well ask it."

Marc stopped and looked at me. It wasn't quite the mussel-cracker face, but he wasn't excited either.

"Okay," I said, coming up with an idea, "how about we

skip rocks on the waves. If mine goes farther, you ask your favor. If yours goes farther, you don't have to."

A smile gradually crossed his face. We used to do this all of the time years ago. Except back then it was to determine if we should eat at Marc's house or mine, or who was going to become the richest when we grew up, or who would have to pick up the dead crab on the beach. "Deal," he said.

I'm pretty good at skipping rocks. I found a round but flat one. The ocean produced the best smooth skipping stones. I angled it sideways so it would hit flat and tried to time it just right between waves. And I totally won. Mostly because a wave caught Marc's rock mid-skip.

He looked up at me, knowing he lost the challenge.

"You can at least ask," I said. "I mean, is it like you need a ride somewhere or help with homework, or you want me to try to fix your Xbox, or you need me to lend you $20?" I was just rambling. More words came out of me than bubbles out of those little treasure chests in aquariums.

"No," he said. He kicked the pebbles a little then said, "I wanted to know if you'd join a swim team with me."

A swim team? That definitely wasn't on my list of favors I guessed he might ask. It took me a moment to even know what to say. "Our school doesn't have a swim team, does it?" I had only been around a little while, but I had never heard of a swim team.

"No," he said, his voice a little quieter than normal, "there's one at the community pool. We'd practice a few times a week and then there are meets and stuff." One of his eyebrows raised while he looked back at me for an answer.

"Why?" I asked, which totally came out wrong. Like I was asking why we would ever want to do that. I quickly tried to clarify. "I mean, why ask me?"

He shrugged, then looked back down at the beach. "I just really need to do something right now. I'm so—" His eyes looked up and off to the side. "I just don't know—" He stopped then started again. "I've just got to get out and *do* something." He shook his fist a little. I hadn't seen him do that before, either. "And I like to swim," he said. "I was just hoping you'd do it with me." He waited another moment. "I don't want to do it alone."

That last part sounded like Marc. I remember him always talking his sister or brother into playing video games with him. I even did it. He hated playing by himself. He never ate alone. He only walked or rode his bike alone if he was meeting up with someone.

"I could probably do that," I said. "But why do you 'need to get out and do something'? Are things bad with your parents or something?" I asked. I know when my parents were going through the divorce, I would just leave the house. I left the house now because of my gigantic stepfamily.

He wrinkled his face for a moment. "Nah, they're great. I just need to do something," he said, and it came out loud and fast, like there was a walrus sitting on him and he needed it off. "I guess life is really stressful. And my grades are tanking. I just need something else to do. Something I might be good at."

I thought about that for a moment. When I lived here before, Marc did have to work really hard in school. I got my good grades pretty easily, but he had to study and study. But his grades never tanked. That would be hard. And he loved to swim. His dad's marina was right on the ocean. (Obviously. It'd be hard for people to bring in their boats if it wasn't.) So we used to play in the ocean just out of the way of the boats. And his family had passes to the community pool so I remember going there with him a few times.

"I really like swimming," I said. I had snorkeled all over the islands and on vacations, looking at cool marine life with my mom. "But I haven't ever raced or anything." I got the nervous minnows swimming through me. Would I be any good?

"Just come with me," he said.

Why ask me and not his other friends? Or maybe he did. Was I just one more he had asked? Were they coming? Or was it just us two going on another adventure, just like old times? Part of me wanted to know, but the other part of me was just glad he asked. "Sure," I said.

He gave me a real smile. Not as big or charming as he used to, but at least it didn't look forced. "Perfect," he said. "Tryouts are tomorrow."

Tomorrow?

What had I gotten myself into?

I felt like a walrus had sat on *me*.

CHAPTER 11

Lizzy

Willa Twitchell, Journal #5,
a week and a half ago

The threadfin butterflyfish is gorgeous. It has alternating black and white lines that mesh in an intricate pattern that then fade into orange and yellow along the tailfin. If you google beautiful fish it will probably pop up. Seriously gorgeous. But there is something about it: maybe the way it sways when it swims. Maybe it's the little pointy snout. I always thought it was snobby. Like it knew it was all that and none of the other fish were as pretty or as smart. And I kind of want an octopus to chase it around just to humble it up.

I've only been back to school for a week, and in my opinion, Lizzy Wallace could use an octopus-chasing too.

"Okay," Mr. Norton said. "You know how this works. You've come prepared with your topic for today. You've thought it out. Now I want to hear both sides of the issue." Mr. Norton taught history, but always spent the first fifteen to twenty minutes talking about current events. He was on a debate kick lately where he'd give us papers to read, then make us argue it out in class.

"Both sides," he repeated. Mr. Norton was not a large man, but with his voice and his unflinching stare, he seemed like one. His nose was a little big for his face and so were his eyes, but that just made him more intimidating. "Don't be like my first-period class and just mention one side."

I had to focus. I liked Mr. Norton. He was fun, in kind of a terrifying way. Like a sea lion. They look so fun and friendly, but if you get close you realize they weigh like 600 pounds and could run right over you. Mr. Norton made us do a lot of homework and he gave a lot of quizzes, but for some reason I still liked him. But that wasn't why I had to focus.

First of all, I had just transferred into this school a few weeks ago. And then I didn't come for a week. I had been in dive-into-a-dark-cave-and-never-come-out mode; a turtle, content inside her shell. I probably never would have come if my new house wasn't so loud and annoying. It was driving me mad. And insanity on top of deep sorrow is a terrible combination. Plus, if a turtle stays in its shell too long, it will just sink in the ocean and starve. So I came to school. And I was still trying to get back on track.

Plus, there was the picture that I put as my phone screen-saver. I've been through every picture on my phone that I had with my mom and I found one that I just couldn't get out of my mind. It was me and Mom at our favorite teppanyaki restaurant, a pretty expensive place. But my mom took me there because I got straight As on my last semester's grades. She kept telling me over and over how proud she was. Grades were important to her. Probably not a surprise that as a scientist she cared about them.

And I had to come through for her. I had to get good grades.

"School uniforms," Mr. Norton said, announcing the topic he had assigned last time. He wrote it quickly on the board and drew a line down the middle of the board just beneath it. "More and more schools throughout the country are requiring them. Tell me the arguments for and against school uniforms." He wrote the word *For* on one side of the board, and *Against* on the other.

I liked talking about issues, but right now, I had so many other things floating around in my head. I would have rather talked about where people go when they die. Or why people let noisy kids completely take over a house. Why I could talk with a humpback whale. Or why I agreed to try out for a swim team when I was probably just going to embarrass myself.

I looked over at Marc. I don't know why, maybe hoping he'd give me some assurance. But he didn't see me. He sat a couple rows over and one behind me. Mr. Norton believed in alphabetical seating charts.

Here was where I showed that I deserved straight As. I had read all of the material that Mr. Norton gave us about school uniforms, preparing for class like I used to when Mom was alive and checking up on me. I raised my hand. Lizzy Wallace's hand shot up too. Of course it did. And if I was being technical, her hand went up before mine. Debate was her thing. Well, one of her things. She might just be good at everything. Plus, her older sister was on the debate team at the high school and Lizzy always found ways of sneaking in that detail in her comments. Mr. Norton called on her first.

"Uniforms can undercut any gang-related behavior in an area," Lizzy said.

Undercut gang-related behavior? Seriously? She spoke like she was reading out of a textbook. Did she memorize those lines to recite them like she was in a play? I mean, we didn't really have any gangs on the island. At least not that I'd ever heard of. She was obviously talking about other places.

Mr. Norton wrote *Stop gang-related behavior* on the *For* side of the board.

Lizzy Wallace had showed up on Tupkuk Island while I was gone and basically filled the top-of-the-class spot. That used to be my spot. If I were a seal, Lizzy would be my orca. Not only was she super annoying, but so far, she got slightly better grades than I did. She asked what I got on the last quiz and the test in math. She's in that class too. At first, I thought she was being friendly, but then she would smile and tell me her score, which was at least a little bit higher. Just plain gloating. And on top of that, she was cute too, always wearing colors that complemented her dark skin. It all made her head more inflated than a pufferfish. If marine biology were a class in school, I would kick her trash right out of the ocean. But it wasn't. Though I really wish it was. I think that would make me feel better.

#MakeMarineBiologyAClass

I still had my hand raised and Mr. Norton called on me.

CHAD MORRIS & SHELLY BROWN

"Uniforms murder self-expression," I said. A short and strong statement. Not bad if I do say so myself. Well, maybe the word *murder* was a little over-the-top. In my study I actually saw and agreed with a lot of reasons for school uniforms, but I wasn't going to be on Lizzy's side.

A murmur of the word *murder* went through the class. But they seemed to like my use of it. Mr. Norton even wrote *Murders self-expression* on the *Against* side of the board.

"And," Nolan said. He was on the basketball team and hardly said a thing unless we were debating something he cared about. Apparently, he cared about uniforms. "Uniforms would be evil. They mean we'd all dress like clones. There would be no style. No showing who we are through what we wear." He said the last sentence louder for emphasis. "With uniforms, you can't wear the clothes that you really want."

I doubt he realized that he basically said the same thing several times. And that it was the same point that I said. But maybe he got the hint when Mr. Norton just put a star next to the words *Murders self-expression*.

"I'm with you," Derrin said. Derrin usually agreed with Nolan, or anyone else who might be a little cooler than he was. "I want to wear my Seahawks jersey." Sounds of approval went through the room. I heard Marc agree. But it was pretty clear that the class didn't want uniforms. Or maybe they really wanted to wear their Seahawks jerseys. Probably both. I'd like to think I started this movement.

"It also means no hats," Talliver said. His name was really

Oliver, but we had two Olivers in our grade. In second grade we started calling the tall one Talliver and the short one Smalliver.

"True," Mr. Norton said. "Though we currently have a no hats policy in our school, so that wouldn't be changing anything."

"And probably no jewelry. No unapproved sneakers," I added.

"Yes. And yes." Mr. Norton said. "But can you give me any more reasons other than the fact that adopting uniforms could limit your self-expression?"

Jarom raised his hand. "Saying 'adopting uniforms' makes them sound like they're puppies."

Mr. Norton didn't write that one on the board. But he did smile. It made me snicker too. Jarom was the class goofball who only spoke when he had a joke.

Lizzy had her hand up again. "I talked to my sister, who's on the state champion debate team. And she had a good point. She said that—" There it was. Took a while this time to bring up her brilliant sister. "—uniforms can discourage bullying. When everyone dresses similar, students tend to get along better."

"That's a good one," Mr. Norton said, jotting another note on the board.

I didn't like that he said Lizzy's point was good. He hadn't said anything like that to me. I tried again.

"Uniforms cost money," I said. "And that means it could force families to spend more money than they have." Mr. Norton jotted down another note, but he didn't tell me it was good.

We chatted about uniforms for another five minutes. Lizzy said uniforms would make it harder to tell who had money and who didn't, and could help us avoid cliques and discrimination.

She claimed it would help kids focus on education. I had heard that too. We obviously read some of the same articles.

But I was glad to wear whatever clothes I wanted. I picked the right side.

And I was glad I was trying hard in class. For Mom.

"Anything else for the against side?" Mr. Norton pointed to *murders self-expression*, which had three stars next to it. I felt like we needed more of an argument. We basically just said the same thing three times and that it cost money. Lizzy had more. And she had said each one like she was the prettiest fish in the ocean.

Mr. Norton clapped his hands. "Alright," he said, signaling the end of this part of class. It depended on how you looked at it. If it was popular opinion, I think I won this one. If it was the number of arguments, Lizzy won. Unfortunately, I think Mr. Norton might have sided with Lizzy.

Ugh. She drove me crazy. I had to beat her at something.

"Let's change things up for the next few weeks," Mr. Norton said. "Next week we are going to start our legitimate debates. I choose the teams. I choose the topics. Two students on one side of the issue. Two on the other." Then he counted us off, so we each had a number between 1 and 23. That's how many people were in my class. I was number 12. Then he pulled out his phone. "Hey, Siri," he said, talking to his phone. "Pick a number between one and twenty-three."

"It's five," Siri said in her electronic voice.

Not me.

I only wanted to debate if I could square off against Lizzy. But number five was Kaycen. He was a quiet kid. Didn't say much.

Mr. Norton asked his phone again. This time Siri picked twenty. Lizzy. She beamed, like she had just been selected for some great honor.

"You two will argue for issue number one on the syllabus," Mr. Norton explained. "And now for the two who will argue against issue number one." He asked his phone again. I really wanted it to be me. Me and Marc. It would be like when we won science fair.

It was two. Jarom. Joking Jarom. Not the best partner. I'd rather have Marc, but I still really wanted to debate against Lizzy.

Mr. Norton asked his phone a final time.

C'mon. C'mon. Pick me. I felt kind of bad about it, because I wanted to work with Marc. Then I could help him with his grades. But I also really wanted to go against Lizzy. "It's twelve," Siri said.

Yes. I almost celebrated out loud. But didn't. I smiled and glanced back at Lizzy. I wanted to give her an I'm-going-to-crush-you look, but still with a cute smile. But Lizzy didn't look at me. She thought she was too good for me.

"Okay," Mr. Norton said. "So Kaycen and Lizzy *for* the issue and Jarom and Willa *against* it."

Jarom called out, "We're going to have Kaycen and Lizzy cream soup next week!" His normal crew laughed at him even though his joke barely made sense.

Mr. Norton kept going like Jarom hadn't said anything. That's the way most of the teachers treated him. "I'll give everyone next class to prepare, then come next week ready to debate. We'll go in numerical order, so topic number one is first and so on. Should we see who is on topic number two?" He put his phone to his mouth and asked for a new number. He went through everyone. Marc got issue number five with Sydney. They would probably do okay.

After a long lecture on the colonization of America, the bell finally rang.

Finally.

I mean it wasn't bad, but it wasn't super interesting either. Definitely not crazy interesting like the tiny Japanese pufferfish that makes amazing symmetrical designs in the ocean floor to attract a girlfriend. Seriously, you should YouTube it. It's a total artist.

Everyone got up and left, but Lizzy actually bumped into me on the way out. Sure, she made it look like an accident, but if it was, she didn't apologize.

I went by Marc's desk as he was still packing up. "Did you see that?" I asked.

"What?" Marc asked. He was about as observant as a cavefish; they don't even have eyes.

"Lizzy just bumped into me," I said.

"It was probably just an accident," he said.

"No," I said, "she was bitter because I actually had some good points today."

Marc just shrugged. Again, a cavefish.

We walked down the hall toward the gym together. And it felt natural. It was what we should be like in middle school. And Marc didn't seem like it bothered him. Maybe he even liked it.

But I wasn't excited for gym. I hated it. Maybe as much as

I hated Lizzy. Marc said he had Spanish. That was an easy A for him; he already spoke fluently. I told him that wasn't fair, but he pointed out that I was taking English, so I stopped arguing with him. Besides, every A he earned would help. Plus, it got him closer to studying computer programming and starting his video game company.

"So," he said, "are you ready for after school today?" He looked like a dolphin about to double flip in front of all his dolphin friends.

I felt the total opposite.

"No," I said, "I'm not even close to ready. I've never raced before, remember?"

"Me neither," he said. "We'll figure it out."

He said "we'll" and my lips curled. Maybe we were becoming friends again.

"Are your other friends coming too?" I asked. "Luke and Nash?" I had been wondering that since last night.

"Nah," Marc said. "They didn't want to."

Inside I sighed in relief. It was just the two of us. It would have been awkward if he was trying to be there as my friend and their friend at the same time. Like he does at lunch sometimes. Plus, if I stunk at it, Luke would probably have made fun of me.

Come to think of it, Marc had probably asked them before me. More than likely, I was the backup plan. Like a serious ocean fisherman who wanted a tuna or a dorado, but settled for whatever he caught. I didn't like that. At all.

But at least I was caught. A back-up plan was still one of the plans.

"Oh," I said, remembering a question I had. "How much does this cost?" My dad had asked this morning when I told him about it.

"Nothing today," Marc said. "And even if we make the team, there are scholarships and stuff."

"Okay," I said. "But if we don't get scholarships, what does it cost?"

"Don't worry about it," Marc said. I hoped he didn't mean he was going to pay for it. I knew his family had the money, but I could handle it.

He didn't actually offer though, and his eyebrows scrunched together in a near musselcracker. I didn't get that.

"We'll deal with that if it comes up," he said. "See ya after school." Then he turned down the hall toward Spanish class.

Deal with it? Like it was a problem? It wasn't a problem. But as I walked to gym and remembered his grumpy face, I wondered if somehow it was a problem for him.

CHAPTER 12

Tryouts

Willa Twitchell, Journal #5, today

Today I felt like a seahorse. Not because they're beautiful and unique and awesome. No. And not because they look so graceful and poised as they swim. Nope. That's not it either. It's because of <u>how</u> they swim. They have a small fin on their back that moves thirty-five to fifty times per second and a pectoral fin by the back of the head that steers. If there was a Guinness Book of World Records for the ocean, they would have an award. The same award I felt like I won today.

"Alright," the coach lady said, her white jumpsuit popping out in contrast to her dark skin. "I'm Trinity Jackson and I oversee this team."

My heart was pounding. Getting Marc back as a friend was worth this, right? I had never done competitive sports before and I felt like a baby porpoise in front of a great white shark.

I reread the text from my mom before I came, the one where she told me that I needed friends. I could do this.

About ten of us stood in a line in our swimsuits. I was wearing my yellow one with black trim. I looked like an electric yellow fish. They have the most brilliant yellow color. Of course, I also looked like a yellow trumpet fish or longhorn cowfish, but those aren't nearly as pretty. Plus, "cowfish" is a terrible name. Who wants to look like a cowfish? Especially since I think they look less like a cow and more like an alien trying to kiss something.

A hand went up somewhere to my left. "Didn't you swim in the Olympics?" a voice asked Coach Jackson. I recognized that voice. I looked down the line and I wanted to float belly-up. Lizzy Wallace. She stood confident, like always. And with her brown skin and white swimsuit, she matched Coach Jackson. She'd probably planned that. I don't know how, but she probably did. I definitely did *not* want Lizzy Wallace with me on the swim team. Could I just quit now?

"It said on the website that you swam in the Olympics twice," Lizzy continued. Looks like she was going to be super chatty here too.

"Yes, I did," Coach Jackson said, a smile slipping across her face.

"Really?" Marc asked. "Like the real Olympics?" He seemed so completely entranced. I couldn't leave, not while he was so excited. And he had been that excited the whole bike ride here.

Coach Jackson's grin got bigger. "Really. The real Olympics." There was something about the way she said it that I knew she was telling the truth. I could tell by the excited murmurs from all the others that we were all pretty impressed. I know I was.

Of course, the fastest human swims something like five miles per hour. When you think about that compared to how we move on land, it's not that fast. Like a jog. A sailfish could thrash that.

"Did you get a medal?" Lizzy asked.

"Nope," Coach Jackson said. "The best I ever got was seventeenth place." I saw a redhead boy mouth "seventeenth" in disbelief. "But that made me the seventeenth-fastest swimmer in the world at the time." She said it with such pride. "And do you know how much time there was between me and the gold medalist?"

I don't think anyone wanted to answer that. I didn't. I thought the answer was probably pretty big and I didn't want her to feel bad.

"Four seconds," she said. "That's it. The gold winner touched, and I . . ." She waited, slowly counting to four. ". . . touched. And that was the difference between first place and seventeenth. Swimming is a sport of seconds."

That was crazy. Four seconds was the difference between the best in the world and someone nobody knew about. That was it.

"Okay," she said, "let's see if you qualify to be on the Tornadoes." She clapped her hands then waved us closer to the pool. But something didn't seem right.

I raised my hand.

"Yes," Coach Jackson said.

"Why are we called the Tornadoes?"

"It's our name," Coach Jackson said, obviously surprised by the question. "That's what the club team is called."

"But it doesn't make sense," I said. "Tornadoes don't swim. I guess they can go over water, but those are called waterspouts. Tornadoes are usually over land."

"But they *are* fast," Lizzy said.

"And scary," a boy I didn't know added.

"But," I said, emphasizing the word so that they would pay attention, "there are so many things that actually swim really fast. We could be the Swordfish, the Flying Fish, the Marlins, or the Orcas."

"True." Coach Jackson smiled, tapping her pen on her clipboard. "We can discuss the name later. For right now, line up in your lanes and let's see you swim the length of the pool."

Somehow I doubted that we would talk about it later.

"Do we have to dive in?" Marc asked, rubbing his hands together.

"Go in however you like," Coach Jackson said. "We'll work on our starts later."

Did Marc not know how to dive? As I thought about it, I hadn't ever seen Marc dive before. He always ran and jumped. Often, he let out a high-pitched scream and flung his arms and legs in every direction until he crashed into the water. But he never dove.

Coach Jackson blew her whistle. "Swimmers, take your mark."

My heart was thrumming faster than a dolphin's tail fin. What if I stunk? What if I was slower than a mola mola? I could just imagine Lizzy laughing at me.

I guess I was about to find out. We all lined up on these little angled stands at the edge of the pool.

I put my toes just over the edge. I think that's how swimmers do it. I hoped that I could beat Lizzy. Or at least not look totally terrible. But that would be so fantastically amazing if I could beat her. I'd put a special journal entry in just for that.

My heart pounded in my chest so fast, I just hoped my arms and legs could do the same.

"Go!" Coach Jackson blew her whistle.

I leaned forward, then pushed off hard with my legs. My body made a spear, my arms extended over my head. After gliding over the pool for who knows how far, I pierced into the water like a harpoon, shooting forward. I probably looked amazing, like poster-worthy. But as I hit the water, I realized I didn't know what stroke I was going to do. Coach hadn't asked for anything specific. Freestyle? Breaststroke? Those were the only two my parents had taught me.

I wished I could swim like a dolphin. Their bodies are round like tubes and their powerful tails swish up and down. Their flukes propel them forward. Or I could swim like a marlin, their large tails pushing from side to side, shooting them through the water. I settled for the front crawl, my arms stretching out in front of me, crashing in over my head as my legs kicked hard. They weren't fins, but they would have to do.

The water was pretty much my life. It was what I loved. My home. I loved being around it. In it. I loved feeling myself move through it. I didn't know exactly how fast I was going, but I was clipping along.

As I turned my head for air, I tried to glimpse where I was compared to the others. I hoped Marc was doing awesome. And I wanted to see Lizzy far behind me. But I didn't see them. It was all a watery mess. Was I way behind? Or in front? So much of me wanted to stop and look around, but that would definitely slow me down. I just pressed forward.

I pushed myself to go faster, moving harder with each stroke. Kicking more. I pictured being a mackerel with a leopard seal on my tail. I had to sprint through the pool.

A few more strokes.

A few more.

Finally, I touched the end of the wall and came up for air. Still panting, I brushed the water off my face and looked around. Someone was behind me and touched the wall. Then someone else. It was like my whole body sighed in relief. I wasn't last.

"Good job, Willa," Marc said. I wiped my face with my hand again and saw him smiling. His big charming smile. Definitely not a grumpy musselcracker. He was loving this. And he didn't have water falling down his face like I did. He had totally beaten me. That was okay. In fact, I was proud of him. I'd have let him win if I knew what I was doing.

"Yeah," Lizzy said in the lane next to Marc. She also didn't have water on her face and had probably been there for a while. She had beaten me too. I was so disappointed I didn't know if I wanted to scream or dart into the cover of an empty wormhole like a goby. "Good job, Willa," Lizzy said with a big smile. But I was sure she didn't mean it. I hadn't beaten her. I didn't even know if I got anywhere close.

Another person hit the wall.

I quickly looked at those I beat. Three. Two girls and a boy. And I think they were all in elementary school. I was basically the slowest of all the middle-schoolers. I was a seahorse, the slowest swimmer in the ocean. A tiny-finned, barely moving seahorse.

"Great job, you guys," Coach Jackson said, clapping a couple more times.

"How did you do?" I asked Marc.

"I got second," he said, his grin just as big as before. It was partly super annoying because I had done so bad. But partly just plain great. He'd said he needed this. Maybe he was right. "Thanks for coming," he said. A soft wave of happiness washed over me.

"Did you beat Lizzy?" I asked, hopefully quiet enough that she couldn't hear.

He looked over his shoulder then nodded.

This wave of happiness was even bigger.

"She got third," he said.

That wasn't good. And I had no idea I was going to be this bad.

"Let's keep warming up," Coach Jackson said.

That was just a warm-up? I had given it all I had and was ready to grab my towel.

"Go ahead and swim back," Coach said.

Swim back. I could do that. And I was determined to do better. Maybe I just got off to a bad start with the first race.

I gave it everything I could—and only beat the elementary school kids again. In fact, I realized that one of the blond boys who had beaten me was still in elementary. I couldn't even beat all of the younger kids.

Coach Jackson showed us how to do the freestyle stroke. I thought I had it down, but she corrected me a couple of times. And when we swam another lap, I barely beat the three I beat before. One of them almost tied with me.

#FeelingSlowerThanASeahorse

"Alright," Coach Jackson said. "Great job today. You swam hard, showed a lot of talent, and a lot of effort. Thank you." She glanced down at her clipboard. Had she written notes about what she was going to say? "We've seen what you can do. If you get a call tonight or tomorrow, you've made the team. If you don't get a call, thanks so much for trying out. Keep swimming and try again next season. Just because you don't make the team this time doesn't mean you're not going to be a great swimmer." Okay, so it was *that* kind of a speech. Basically, she was saying that we were all amazing, but if we got a call today or tomorrow, then we were more amazing than the others.

Marc's big smile hadn't changed. It was like his Xbox was back, but better than before. But when he looked at me, his grin wavered just for a second. He was probably thinking what I was thinking. He was in. But was I? And I wasn't sure what I wanted. I mean, I wanted Marc back as a friend. I wanted to hang out with him, and although coming to swim practice a couple times a week wasn't my first choice, it was something. I wouldn't be in my room all shelled up. And I'd be doing what I thought my mom wanted.

But if I didn't make the team, then Marc would be busy and I'd be alone.

I tried to smile back.

CHAPTER 13

Focus

Willa Twitchell, Journal #5, today

Whales migrate. The gray whale swims thousands of miles from Mexico to the Arctic every migration. It's like me going from Tupkuk Island to Tokyo and back again. But they swim it. Of course, they have to watch out for the orcas, their scheming, conniving, maniacal enemy. To stay safe, the gray whales hug the coast most of the way, but at Monterey Bay they have to cross open waters and there is a huge gorge beneath. It opens up for miles beneath them. And that's the best place for a killer whale ambush. The gray whale can't even see it coming.

School is like crossing a big unprotected gorge. And today I was ambushed. Stupid Lizzy Wallace.

I glanced over at Jarom, my debate partner, at the computer next to me. "Are you even studying?"

"Of course," Jarom said. "Check it out." He tilted his screen to show some cannon he was blasting at a space monster.

He was going to get us both in trouble. "C'mon," I said. "Focus."

"I am," he said. "This isn't easy." He clicked a few more times. "I also checked my *Battle-Ax Brawl* score and I'm crushing it. Seriously, Derrin doesn't stand a chance."

Earlier in class, Mr. Norton had asked Lizzy if she was going to be ready next time for the debate. She said, "Definitely," and nodded big. I hated the way she said it. It was like she thought she already had the debate won. She probably thought she did. And I really wanted to beat her.

I still couldn't get what she did to me earlier in the class out of my head. She came into class all happy and said hi to me, and she seemed really nice. But then she said it was nice to see me yesterday at swim practice. And she said it with a face that said she knew she was such a better swimmer. And then, as if that wasn't enough, she mentioned that she got a call that she made the team. Of course, she then asked if I did. It was a total set up. Like orcas appearing out of the gorge. She knew she was a better swimmer than me; she was rubbing my face in it. I felt completely attacked.

I couldn't think of the right way to react. There wasn't anything to do to fight back. Like a gray whale in the same situation, I just tried to roll with it and survive. So I told the truth; I shook my head and said that I hadn't gotten a call. Then she acted surprised . . . like this wasn't all part of her plan. She even apologized, but I doubt she really meant it.

That just made me want to win this debate more.

But after asking Lizzy if she was ready for the debate, Mr. Norton asked me. I liked that. It was like he recognized me as the other unofficial team captain. It was really going to be a showdown between me and Lizzy. I tried to sound just as confident, and I think I nailed it. I hope I did.

Now Jarom and I had work to do. "I meant focus on our debate," I said, shaking my finger over his game.

"I already did that," Jarom said. "We have the easier side. All the research is basically just helping us win."

He was right. From what I'd seen, there was study after study feeding us everything we needed to take down the Lizzy-Kaycen team.

Our debate question was about whether screen time was good for children. And we had the side arguing that it wasn't good. Easy, right? Adults harass us about it all the time. All we had to do was parrot back all of the things that they say to us:

It's a poor use of time.

Zombifies our brains.

Leads to lack of focus.

Leads to obesity.

We can become addicted.

It's bad for social skills.

It can encourage violent behavior.

We've all heard them. All that Jarom and I had to do was find all the studies to back them up. "Show me what you've got," I said, coming up behind him and looking at his screen where multicolored aliens were shooting oversized cannons at each other.

"Just a minute." Jarom made the whole screen flip to another point of view. The motion made me a little sick. "I've got to finish this level to save my progress."

"So," I said. "Because you're addicted to video games, you can't help me research why playing video games is bad."

"Ouch," Jarom said sharply, not because he was upset with me, but because he just got shot. "C'mon," he said, his avatar frantically running away from the big red lanky alien that was chasing him with a giant blue blaster gun. "What were you saying?" he asked.

"Never mind."

"We all play video games," Jarom said, trying to pretend like he had been listening to me. "Not liking video games is like not liking the Seahawks."

The kids in my class were obsessed with that football team. I didn't play video games or watch the Seahawks. "Did you know," I asked, "that there isn't really even a bird called the seahawk? Some people guess they could be named after the osprey or skua, but there isn't really a seahawk." He didn't answer so I kept on. "It doesn't make sense. Plus, if there was, it couldn't play sports."

"What?" Jarom said, saving his level. When he finished, he spun in his chair to face me. "They could catch a ball in their talons." Then he made some cawing sound, like he was a seahawk, I guess.

Everyone looked over.

I shook my head. "Let's just get back to the debate."

"There isn't anything else to do," Jarom said. "Took me thirty seconds to find this article and it lists all of the reasons for us." He pulled up an article from *The Social Blast* that listed ten reasons kids should lower their screen time.

"That's all you have?" I asked. At first his confident attitude calmed me a little, but now it just ticked me off. "I know this debate seems simple, but we both know Lizzy will have researched everything. And there has to be a reason why this is even a debate. There has to be another side. It's not like she's just going to say, 'Screen time is so much fun, so we should do as much as we want.' If we haven't really researched it, then Lizzy is going to tear us apart."

"Tear us apart?" he asked. "You almost made debate sound interesting for a second." The pads of his fingers softly tapped his keyboard while we talked. Not enough to actually type anything. But just the right amount to drive me batty.

"Thanks," I said, surprised he'd complimented me.

"I said 'almost,'" Jarom clarified, stretching.

I blew a strand of hair out of my eyes and pointed at his screen. "Please, find me five more articles like that one. Write down the things they say to support our position."

"Wow, Bossypants," Jarom said, "take your boiling pot off the stove." I wasn't really sure what that meant. But he turned and started working, so mission accomplished.

I did the same. I read and I logged notes. I jotted down ideas. I was on research fire. But after so long, my mind drifted to Marc, who was working on the computer on the other side of me. I kept glancing at him. He was frowning and rubbing his forehead.

I thought I knew why. And we'd have to talk about it sooner or later. I looked down at my fingers on the keyboard and started. "So," I said, "you got the call, right? You're on the team?"

"Yeah," he said, his frown becoming deeper. "I heard you tell Lizzy that you haven't. I'm really sorry."

There. We said it. And at least he was sad that I didn't make it. Of course, that didn't mean I wasn't fighting to keep my face from going crimson. "You don't have to feel bad," I said, trying hard to look happy and not jealous or self-conscious, or wishing desperately that I could disappear. "You earned it."

That was a pretty good answer under the circumstances.

I also felt a little betrayed. People are always saying how great it is to try new things, to put yourself out there. And then something like this happens and you aren't any good and you wish you never tried. But I faked it okay.

"But I don't want to do swim team by myself," he said. Was he serious, or just being nice? He sounded serious. "Maybe you'll still get the call. Coach said she'd make the calls over two days. Tonight is still a possibility."

I guess technically it could happen, but why would she call some last night and wait on the others until today? That didn't really make sense. That ship had already sailed. That flotilla of turtles had already migrated. "Maybe," I said.

"Hey, Willa," Jarom whisper-shouted next to me. "Focus!"

I looked at him, then his computer, then back at him. *Really?* I pointed to an armadillo right as it popped its gun and confetti burst across the screen. I guess he'd just started a new game. Marc could design a better game than that.

"No time for chitty-chat," Jarom said. "We've got a debate to win."

I turned back to Marc. "Just text me later," he said. "If you get the call or not, I want to know." And even though I knew it was only going to end in a pity text, it was okay. At least he cared.

CHAPTER 14

Backflip for Me

Willa Twitchell, Journal #5, today

I talked to Meg again today. I know. I know. You're probably sick of hearing about that, but it's so incredible every time. I'm still not sure how it even works. I did some more research to try and figure it out and this is what I learned: For humpbacks, most of the complicated songs are sung by the males. A group of them will all sing the same song that can be heard for twenty miles from each singer. The song changes and they all change with it. It blows my mind. What would it be like to be so connected to others? To be singing the same song? Meg and I aren't male humpbacks and we don't even know any of the same songs. (Though it might be fun to teach her "Baby Shark.") But we are connected. And I hope it never ends. I think I need it.
    #TotallyKiddingAboutBabyShark

#ThatSongWouldPolluteTheOcean
#AndNowItsInMyHead

~~~~~~~~~~~~~~~~

"So, what do you do with a scurnal?" Meg asked. Talking with Meg was easier this time. It was like finding the wifi sweet spot in your house. I knew how close I should stand to the water and I got better at hearing her.

"It's a *journal*," I corrected. After dinner I had snuck out back to the beach and was sitting on the rocks, dangling my feet in the water, trying not to think about the fact that no one had called about swim team. "And you write in them. Well, *you* wouldn't, but I do." I couldn't picture a whale jotting down her thoughts with a pen between her fins. I wondered if Meg even knew what writing was. "Writing, it's—" I started to explain.

"When you make scratches on something so that you will always remember that it happened, right?" Meg answered. "I do learn some things from the people I see."

I was impressed.

No one was around and the sun was going down soon. I tried to finish up my entry while I could still see it.

The water lapped at my toes—in and out, in and out. Meg spoke up again, "How did your swimming thing go?"

"It wasn't—" I started, but then caught myself. "Wait. How did you know?" I hadn't told her about swim team at all. "Oh," I said, realizing what happened, "you were . . ." I was about to say "eavesdropping," but I was pretty sure a whale wouldn't understand that word. "You were listening to us?"

Meg gave her bubble chuckle. "You were having your whole

conversation right by the ocean." She was right. I beat Marc at rock skipping and our whole chat was right by the waves.

I've heard kids get all conspiratorial about the fact that their home AI or their phones can always hear them. That's nothing compared to the idea that all of those sea creatures with great hearing are listening in on everyone's conversations near the ocean. Thank goodness they're not spies for the government.

At least I didn't think they were.

"Swim didn't go great," I said. "I'm not very fast."

"Maybe I can teach you," Meg sang said. "I am kind of an expert. And I can swim faster than boats."

Swimming lessons from a humpback whale sounded absolutely epic. But I doubted that everything would transfer over to a human. "I'd love some pointers," I said. "But you'll have to remember that I am a different species. I'm a lot shorter and lighter. And my body doesn't move like yours." I was about seventy-six feet shorter, and thirty-three tons lighter. But I didn't bring that up.

Meg agreed.

"It was good to go, anyway," I said. "To show Marc that I want to be his friend again." I quickly added, "and just his friend. No lip smacking." I heard a melodious chuckle come from the water. "But," I scooped up some rocks off the ground and sifted through them for shells, "Marc made the team, and I didn't."

Meg waited for a moment. "I don't know what that means." That took a while to explain, but eventually Meg got it. "So, it's like you humans put yourselves in pods, but don't let other humans in."

"Yeah, if you're not good enough," I said.

I could almost hear Meg thinking. "You are strange, strange creatures."

"I guess," I said. And I spilled out everything about Lizzy too. I think all the sadness from mourning my mother took up almost all of the space inside of me; I didn't have room to harbor all of these other feelings. So I dumped them on Meg.

"Lizzy is like a bottom feeder of the ocean," Meg said, trying to summarize what I said. "Like a cuttlefish that has hypnotized other people into thinking she's amazing, but she's really terrible and lethal."

"I think you got it," I said.

"Except she's your same species," Meg said.

"Yeah," I said. But that felt a little strange. She was my same species.

"I have the perfect story for you," Meg said.

I closed my journal. "Okay," I said, "hook me up."

She paused then said quite seriously, "Hook you up? Like bait?"

"No," I said, having not even thought about it, "it means you're going to give me something. In this case a story."

"You humans use your words so oddly," she said. Then her voice became cheery again. "Anyway, when I was up north, a few migrations ago, we came upon these orcas who had bullied a seal onto a small slab of ice. They circled the ice, even breaking pieces off, trying to get to the seal. When they couldn't reach it, they got diabolical. Two of them swam together, causing a wave that washed over the ice and almost carried that poor seal into the ocean. Another orca was waiting on the other side."

"That's so mean and smart—but really just mean," I said. I think I just found a new nightmare. The idea was terrifying.

"Oh, it made me so mad," Meg said. "That seal wouldn't have made more than a snack for one of them. And to taunt and torture it. It upset me. So my friend and I headed straight for them."

Charging orcas? This story was intense.

"Again, the orcas swam together," Meg continued. "But this time, four of them swam in a line. The wave would be huge and the seal would definitely wash off the ice." I could imagine the whole terrible situation. "My friend raced closer. The wave hit the seal and it didn't have a chance. But as the seal slid off the ice, my friend pushed himself between the seal and an orca. He spun onto his back, reached out a pectoral fin, and scooped the seal onto his upturned belly."

"Whoa," I said. #HeroHumpback

"The orcas didn't quit, but rammed right into my friend's side in hopes of dislodging the seal from his spot on my friend's belly. But my friend kept going. Still floating on his back, he filled his chest with air and raised that seal clean out of the water to a height the orca could never reach him."

"That's amazing," I said.

"Yeah," Meg agreed. "Now, my friend wasn't the bravest humpback in the ocean. When he was little, he was terrified of orcas. But he carried that seal until the orcas gave up. Then he dropped the frightened thing off on an ice shelf that gave him plenty of room to get away to safety.

"When I asked him what made him so brave," Meg continued, "he said that he wasn't really thinking about what would happen to him if he got involved. But he couldn't stop asking himself what would happen to that seal if he *didn't* get involved."

After a pause, I realized that was the end of the story. "That was really cool," I said. "But what does it have to do with what we were talking about?"

Meg got quiet then gave a melodious giggle. "Um," she said, "yes, I had a great point."

"Maybe because Lizzy is an orca?"

"Yes," Meg said. "That's it. Maybe she *is* an orca, but that doesn't mean you can't get involved. Don't let her intimidate you. Help others. Think about how you could make a difference."

A pep talk about whales and orcas from a whale. Nice. That was my language. "Thanks," I said. I really did feel better. Maybe I shouldn't let Lizzy get to me.

"Sure thing," Meg said. "When you swim from one side of the great ocean to the other, you're bound to have a story or two."

My phone rang. "Just one second," I said. "My phone . . . my rectangle is, um . . . signaling me." It wasn't always easy to speak in a way Meg could understand. I turned away from the ocean trying not to be rude. "Hello," I said.

"Hello," the person on the other line said. "This is Coach Jackson down at the Tupkuk Island Community Pool. Is this Willa Twitchell?"

"Yes," I said, my heart suddenly pumping a decillion times a second. It was probably almost as bad as the seal trapped on the ice.

Okay. Maybe not that bad, but it was pounding.

Coach Jackson continued, "I'm just calling to let you know that you made the Tornados. Congratulations." It sounded like she had been saying this almost word for word over and over again since yesterday. There wasn't much enthusiasm. But I didn't care. I think my heart almost floated out of me, and my brain rocketed through four different thoughts one right after the other:

1. *I made it. I was good enough. Phew. Phew. And phew again.*
2. *Take that, Lizzy Wallace. Take your smug little questions and shove them in the toilet. I'm the humpback that stopped your orca attack.*
3. *But I wasn't that good of a swimmer. What did that say about the team? Did they take everyone? And was I going to be on the team just to mess up in meets and bring everyone down?*
4. *But still . . . take that, Lizzy Wallace.*

"We'll have our next practice on Monday," Coach Jackson said. "I look forward to seeing you there."

"I'll be there," I said. As I hung up, it felt like I was riding the biggest wave in the world and it wasn't going to ever come crashing down. I gave out a happy yell over the ocean.

"What did your rectangle say?" Meg asked.

"I made the team!" I shouted.

Meg gave a musical hurrah, then I imagined that she did a huge back flop. I mean, I couldn't see her from where I was.

And she did it just for me.

CHAPTER 15

Like a Wave Flung Me into a Coral Reef

Willa Twitchell, Journal #5, today

The Great Pacific Garbage Patch, or sometimes called the trash vortex, is where the currents take a lot of the junk that people throw into the ocean. It's between California and Hawaii and about three times the size of France. Some of it is plastics that break down into tiny pieces over time. And then they can end up in animals' bodies.

Whales, dolphins, sea turtles, and lots of birds migrate through the garbage patch. That worries me.

And sometimes it feels like I'm going through a garbage patch too.

I texted Marc.

> I made the team!!!!! 🎉

99

Though I was definitely conflicted on how good this actually was, I had something I was going to do with Marc. Something went right. Maybe the universe didn't hate me. I was getting my friend back. We were going to hang out twice a week and every now and then on nights and Saturdays when we had meets.

I found myself pedaling my bike back home a lot faster than I usually do. And I was going uphill.

It was like when I just got my grades and had proof that I had earned straight As. My mom was so proud. Or when I decided that I should buy the milk we needed from the grocery store in Japan on my way home from school. And I spoke to the cashier in my broken Japanese and totally got the job done—by myself. I had done it. I tried it and it worked. My mom loved that too. Or when we were diving at Senjojiki Beach and I found a feather star. It wasn't swimming, but I saw it even before the world's leading authority on the species. That one felt extra good.

My phone buzzed. I waited to check it until I reached the house.

Very cool. Gonna be fun!

I wished he would have said that he always knew I'd make it, or thanks for really putting myself out there just for him. But "Gonna be fun," was something. And I hoped it would be fun.

I parked my bike in the shed and rushed to the house. But as soon as I walked through the door, my wave crashed. It crashed and threw me against a coral reef. Like a surfer going in the wrong direction.

I saw Masha sitting on the sofa looking at her phone.

Masha.

Not Mom.

Somehow, somewhere in my mind, I actually expected Mom to be there. To be excited to hear my news.

How had that gotten into my head? Just because I had accomplished something? My mom and I hadn't lived in this house for years. But somehow, I had expected her, or hoped for her, or my heart knew how much I counted on her that it forgot.

Everything drained out of me, like I was a squeezed sponge. I wanted to disappear. Not like run away or sneak back out to the beach. Just disappear. Just dissolve. Just be anywhere but here.

"Willa, where have you been?" Masha asked, after finally looking up from her phone. "I thought you were upstairs."

Part of me wanted to answer, but it was just the smallest part. Another part of me wanted to scream at Masha for not being my mom. Why was she on our couch? Why wasn't she in some different home and why wasn't my mom here? Maybe if we hadn't left Tupkuk Island, then we would have gotten Mom to the doctor's office fast. Or maybe Dad would have seen warning signs and we could have stopped it. Anger filled me. On some level I knew it didn't make sense at all, but it was real to me.

I didn't answer and ran upstairs. As soon as the door clicked behind me, I clenched my fists and whisper-screamed. Every emotion locked in my heart, or bones, or floating under my skin tried to shoot out. I wanted to cry and punch and scream and fade into silence. I wanted to explode. To melt. To rocket away. All at once.

Instead, I just stood there. Like a statue. Like a memorial to nothing. Like I had been turned to stone.

Knock-knock.

I couldn't even respond.

My dad opened the door anyway. "Where have you been?" my dad asked, his words loud and upset. Plus, with his beard he seemed a little angrier all the time.

"I . . ." I didn't want to break down, or scream. I could hear my heart beating in my ears. Everything in me pounded. Quick breath. I could do this without bursting at him. "I went down to the beach." My voice came out steadier than I expected.

"What were you doing down there alone?" my dad asked. His voice was gruff and abrupt.

Seeing him mad funneled all my emotions into anger. "I need to be there to . . ." Then I couldn't finish. The anger flooded over my brain. Why was he angry at me? Why wasn't he upset about Mom? Why didn't he walk into every room of this house missing her? Like me.

"You didn't ask," he said, stern. "I need to know where you are."

I thought about telling him that I had gone several times this week and he hadn't noticed. I just forgot to sneak back in tonight. But I didn't want him to know so I let the anger sink enough for me to calmly say, "Sorry." I didn't mean it. I just didn't want to fight right now.

"And. . . ." His eyebrows raised. He was about to lecture me hard.

But I just looked down, trying not to cry. Moments ago, I was hoping to tell Mom my good news. Now this.

My dad looked at me, but didn't say anything.

And then Masha was there, right inside the doorway. She launched into all the same questions about where had I been, and the same statements about how I couldn't be down at the beach alone and I had to ask permission. At one point she got loud enough that Hannah started to cry from her room. Then Masha looked at me like it was my fault.

But then my dad jumped in. "Willa just needed some space," he said.

What was that?

Masha looked at him and then at me. Was he on my side now?

"You need to be more obedient and more careful," Masha said, and gave an exaggerated nod. I didn't say anything. I didn't want to. "Everyone else is in bed," she added. "You should be, too." She left, probably to go get Hannah who was awake now, though it wasn't my fault.

My dad stayed in the doorway.

I just stood there. And then he walked over and gave me a hug. A big lumberjack hug. Except I always pictured lumberjacks as huge musclemen. My dad was a little mushy around the middle. But I didn't care. I got lost in it. And then tears came and my legs got weak. And he just squeezed tighter. And I think I cried more.

He whispered, "I miss her too."

CHAPTER 16

News

Willa Twitchell, Journal #5, today

Different kinds of Cephalopods ink; octopi, squid, and cuttlefish all shoot out a dark substance from an ink sac between their gills. The inks are different colors, black to more bluish to brown. The idea is that the ink makes like a smokescreen so they can escape from predators. But you have to admit that a distraction of ink is cooler than smoke any day. The ink might also have some chemical qualities that throw off the predator as well. I'm sure predators feel really stupid when they think they've got their prey, but it slips away. That happens to me sometimes. Not that I'm a predator, but something I really wanted sometimes slips right past me. And sometimes it happens to a friend. Marc got inked and I'm not sure what to do about it.

"Hey, Masha," I said, pulling two slices of bread out of a bag. She glared at me a little. She didn't like that my dad gave me permission to make a snack after school. She kept a tight rein on all the food for her kids. "I just wanted to remind you that I have swim practice today." After last night, I was trying to be nicer to her and make sure she knew where I was going. And I liked saying it. Being on the swim team sounded so good. My insides were bubbling like lava out of the ocean floor, both from nerves and excitement.

"What?" she asked, then processed what I had said. "Okay." She just didn't have the energy to worry about me. She was always chasing kids and changing diapers and making meals. I went from having a mom who was my best friend and I was hers to having a mom who checked in every now and then.

"Swimming!" Nadia said. "I wanna go. I wanna go." She had been in the next room, but apparently heard me. And then she pretended to swim around the room, her arms whirling in big circles, her blonde pigtails bouncing. She looked more like a moving windmill than a swimmer. Garth followed her example, but more awkwardly.

"Shhhh," Masha said, "you'll wake Hannah." She said it like waking Hannah was like killing off the last hawksbill turtle. I think Masha spent half her life trying to keep Hannah sleeping.

"Hey," Nadia said, fake swimming up next to me. She looked at what was in my hands, then up to my face. "I want a sandwich too." I had just thrown tomatoes and lettuce between my slices of bread.

Masha glared at me like I just caused an oil spill. I was in danger of causing two huge crises in ten seconds. "Nope," she said, speaking to Nadia. "You've already had a snack."

"But a sandwich is better," Nadia said.

"Sandwich, sandwich," Garth repeated.

Masha rolled her eyes. She was even better at that than glaring.

"Better go," I said, slapping the meat on my sandwich, throwing everything back in the fridge and getting out of there before Masha could look at me like I'd drained the whole ocean.

As I walked out the front door, I almost stepped on Caleb. He was sitting on the doorstep. "Sorry, Caleb," I said, stumbling past him.

He looked up at me, then my sandwich. Here we go again. I started to leave before he could make a big deal.

"I followed you to the beach yesterday," he said quietly.

I stopped. That didn't have anything to do with my sandwich. And I didn't like the idea of my seven-year-old stepbrother at the ocean by himself. He didn't know what I knew. I remember how mad Masha got at me. I could only imagine how angry she'd get at Caleb. Then again, he was probably making this up.

"Pretty sure I would have seen you," I said cocking my head in disbelief.

"I was hiding," was his only answer.

"Don't go down there anymore," I said. "It's dangerous."

He didn't respond. He was probably sitting on the doorstep because he was in some sort of trouble. Best to let him be.

I ran over to get my bike from the shed. "And don't follow me to the pool," I shouted over my shoulder as I jumped on and pedaled away.

Soon I was near sailfish speed. I'd been biking twice after school today, trying to get in better shape for swim. I met up with Marc and we both rode our bikes to practice.

When I got there, someone other than my stepmother tried to kill me with their eyes. Well, to be fair, at first Lizzy looked at me in total confusion. Then realization. Then a glare.

I've never been prouder to be standing anywhere in an electric yellowfish swimsuit.

"Welcome, Tornadoes," Coach Jackson said. "You've made the team!" She said it like it was some sort of great accomplishment. And I felt it. I looked down the line to see who else made it. Then I looked again. Were there the same amount of people as last time?

"Did you cut anyone?" Lizzy asked, apparently realizing the same thing.

"Everyone made the minimum requirements," Coach Jackson said.

Great. Now my accomplishment wasn't really an accomplishment.

"We timed all of you," Coach Jackson said, "and you all were within the range of a new swimmer for your age and height. Plus, it's good practice to go through tryouts like you will if you go on further with swim."

I think I heard Lizzy sigh.

"I'll be timing you more," Coach Jackson said. "We have our first meet in two weeks. And then you get to see not only how fast you are compared to each other, but how fast you are against another team. It should be challenging and fun."

I think she believed it, but I didn't. My insides flubbed like a spineless sea blob. Unless I improved a lot, I would be losing to most of my team and strangers with an audience looking on.

Yay.

Forty-five minutes later, practice was over. I definitely wasn't sure it was a good thing that I made it. I didn't do any better. I always came in close to last. Always. Lizzy did really well, almost giving Marc a run for the second spot. But then he also did a good job of catching up to the girl with the sandy blonde hair who kept winning. Those three seemed to be pushing each other to be faster and faster. I really wished I was one of them. Of course, Lizzy took every opportunity to look over at me after a lap to make sure it was clear that I wasn't on her same level. When she saw me looking at her, she even gave one of her gloating smiles.

At the end of practice, Coach Jackson sent us to change but said she wanted to talk to us before we went home. When I walked out of the locker room to meet Marc, Lizzy had beat me out. And she was standing right next to him, laughing at something he had said.

Now she was trying to steal my friends.

"Hey, Willa," Marc said and waved me over. I didn't want to join him, not if she was there.

"I don't even like raisins," Marc said, and raised his fingers. "Now all my fingers look like them."

Lizzy laughed again. I guess they were talking about water-wrinkled fingers.

I stood next to them both, confused. Why was Lizzy hanging out here? Marc was *my* friend. Not hers. And how could Marc be talking to her and joking around? He knew she was a despicable bottom feeder.

"I hope we become immune eventually," Lizzy said, looking at her own pruney hands.

I had no idea what to say. But I wanted to say something that was better than what Lizzy said. I could spurt out facts about humpbacks or dolphins or crabs, but I didn't think that would do much good.

"Are you ready for our debate tomorrow?" Lizzy asked me. And she asked it like she was ready and even if I thought I was ready, I wouldn't be nearly as ready as she was.

"Yeah," I lied. I still had to study up tonight.

"Me too," she said and smiled an evil, I-want-to-eat-you-alive smile.

"Okay," Coach Jackson said. I hadn't seen her come out. She was still wearing her swimsuit, though she never actually swam with us. And when she stood out in the lobby with the rest of us in regular clothes, she seemed out of place. "Gather around." She waited for us to obey. "So here is your info packet," she said, and began handing out large envelopes. "Inside are copies of the swimming regulations, the schedule, and the cost of being on the team." I opened my envelope and started to thumb through it. "Let me know if you have any questions."

I looked through everything for a minute like everyone else, but wanted to get out of there. I had to get back home to study for the debate tomorrow. Coach Jackson dismissed us so I turned to Marc. "Ready to go?" I asked.

"Give me a minute," he said, watching a few of the others

who started asking Coach Jackson questions. "I'll meet you outside." Was that a hint? Like he didn't want me around? Before I had time to react, he turned to Lizzy. "See you next time, Lizzy." At least he was brushing her off too.

I waited, trying to figure out what he was doing, but when he saw me, he repeated. "Seriously, I'll catch up. I just need to ask a question." He was definitely trying to get rid of me.

I went outside and watched in through the big glass doors. Thankfully, Lizzy left. Marc waited until no one else was there, then approached Coach Jackson. He pointed at his packet then asked a question. What had he waited so long to ask about? What did he not want the rest of us to hear?

Wait. I had an idea. Coach had mentioned the cost for being on the team. I had asked that before and Marc told me it wouldn't be a problem because they had scholarships. I bet he was asking about them. But why all the secrecy? And was he asking for me? Maybe he thought that since I just lost my mom we could use the help.

Sweet, but I'd be okay.

Last time the subject had come up, I told him that I could pay for myself, didn't I? I wasn't sure, but I did remember his grumpy musselcracker face.

Coach Jackson shook her head. Marc asked something else and she shook her head again. I couldn't hear it all, but if that was what he was asking about, I didn't think they did scholarships anymore.

From the look on Marc's face as he walked back toward me, it was like he just got inked by an octopus.

"You okay?" I asked.

His jaw was tight. "I don't think I can swim," he said flatly.

What? Why couldn't he swim? What had he been asking about? "Why?" I asked.

Marc pounded his fist into his open palm. I had never seen him do that before. He let out a low growl, but didn't answer my question.

I didn't know what to do. Should I ask again, or just let him keep punching himself? He looked up at me, then punched a couple more times. "It's just my family doesn't . . ." he stopped himself. "We've had to spend a lot on . . ." He didn't finish but pounded his fist a few more times. I hung there in silence, waiting to see what he would say.

He didn't say anything.

I didn't really understand what was wrong. It sounded like money was a problem. But that couldn't be it. His family was well off. But just in case, I thought I'd offer to help. "I can talk to my dad, and maybe we could pay for—"

"Don't," Marc said, loud and forceful. It was like a command from an emperor.

"Really, I think that maybe—" I tried again.

"I said *don't*," Marc repeated. Full-on black musselcracker.

Then we got on our bikes and he didn't say a thing as we rode together.

Just like that I was pretty sure swimming and hanging out with Marc a couple times a week was gone.

CHAPTER 17

Carry

Willa Twitchell, Journal #5, today

The Mariana Trench is the deepest, darkest trench in the ocean. You could put Mount Everest in it and it would still be covered by over two miles of water. The pressure is 1,000 times more than at the surface. I think I know what that feels like.

~~~~~~~~~~

"Meg," I called out, running down to the surf, "are you around?" Of course, she didn't answer quickly—but she never did.

"Willllla," she eventually called back, her voice as melodious as ever. "Good to hear from you. How was your swimming game?"

I caught my breath. "Swim team practice? It was . . . fine. I liked it." I tried to sound more positive than I felt. She sounded so happy for me. But I was still thinking about what had just happened with Marc after practice.

"Of course you did," Meg sung out loud and deep. I guess that was the humpback way of celebrating. "Good job, little human. You *boulder*!"

"Thanks," I said. "But what does 'you boulder' mean?"

"You know," Meg said. "For some reason when you humans do something really impressive, you say, 'You boulder!' I don't know why. Do you just like rocks? It doesn't make sense to me."

"We don't say that," I said. "We don't . . . Oh." Realization swept over me. "You mean that I *rock*."

"Rock. Boulder. Same thing," Meg said, her voice a little flat with confusion.

"No," I said using a stick to brush aside a bunch of seaweed that had crowded a small pool, "'you rock' makes sense. 'You boulder' doesn't."

"It's the same thing," Meg insisted. "How could it not make sense?"

"I don't know," I said. "But we only say one of them. Anyway, I can't stay long, Meg." I had stopped in for just a few minutes on my way home from swimming.

"Oh, that's too bad," Meg said, her song going a little sad. "I like our talks."

"I'm just stressed out right now," I said. "I've got my big debate tomorrow so I have to go home and study a lot."

"The one where you are going to beat the bottom-feeder?" Meg asked.

"Yes, exactly," I said. "And on top of that, something went

wrong at swim practice today and I don't think Marc's going to go back."

"But you both just started," Meg said.

"I know," I said. "I think it has to do with some secret he's keeping from me."

Meg waited for a moment. "Keeping secrets doesn't sound good," Meg said. But by the way she paused I could tell she was going to say something else. "But what is a secret?"

"You don't know what a secret is?" I groaned. This was not going to be as quick of a trip as I wanted. Talking to a whale was hard sometimes.

"Um, no," Meg said. "I guess we don't have those in the ocean."

"Sure, you do," I said. "It's like an anglerfish with its light in the deepest parts of the ocean." We had already talked about anglers. "Fish get attracted to it, but the secret is that behind the light is a fish that wants to eat them. That's a secret. It's something that others don't know." I glanced out over the water at the sun getting closer to the horizon. It sent out beautiful reds and golds across the water.

"Oh . . ." Meg said. "Are you saying that Marc is trying to eat you? That doesn't sound like a very good friend at all."

"No. No. No," I said, taking off my sandals and stepping into the water as another wave lapped up on the beach. "I didn't explain that well. It's not like that. It's like I see that there's a light, but I'm not sure if it's a good light or a bad light."

"I'm not sure what you're doing in the deepest parts of the

ocean," Meg said, her song confused again. "The pressure down there would kill you. It would probably kill me."

"I'm not in the deepest part of the ocean," I said. This was getting tricky. "Forget the anglerfish. Marc knows something and he won't tell it to me. And I just want to know because if he needs help, I want to help." I still couldn't imagine why he wouldn't be able to pay for the swim team. *If* that even was the problem. Maybe it was just that his parents were making him earn it and he didn't have enough time.

"Oooooh," Meg said. "But if I understand this right, sometimes I think you're keeping a secret from me."

"What?" I asked, stepping out of the water. Where did that come from? It was like a Pacific Ocean perch swam past me out of nowhere.

"Something is bothering you, Willa," Meg explained. "Something that you haven't quite told me about. I think you've almost said it a couple of times, but you haven't. Maybe it's just because we've been interrupted. Or maybe you don't tell me about it because you don't think a whale could understand. But if I can, I would like to help."

I didn't say anything. The stings crept across my body. They started at my feet and then ran up until I was almost trembling with the pain. It was like a cone snail. They can sting, poison, paralyze, and then eat their prey whole.

"Maybe I'm like you," Meg said. "I just want to help my friend with their secret."

I waited a second, letting that sink in.

"You're right," I said. And then before I thought about it

anymore, before I kept it all inside anymore, I just let it burst out of me. I didn't want to be swallowed by it. "Meg, my mom died." I wanted to say more, it just wasn't quite coming. I closed my eyes. "And I miss her, all the time."

Everything went quiet.

The waves still rolled in and out and birds still flew overhead, but silently. Like time stopped.

At least that's how it felt.

It was good and terrible at the same time. Like I was brave. Like the words were swimming in truth. But also, like it made it more real. And that brought the emptiness as wide and deep and dark as the Mariana Trench.

"Oh, Willa," Meg said, "I'm so sorry." And she let out a long mournful call.

I listened as the moan went on. It was lower and trembled. And I liked that about it. "Yeah," I said, "I'm sorry too."

More silence.

"At times like this," Meg said, "we humpbacks swim close to one another to let each other know that we are right here. I wish we could do that. I think you humans wrap your fins around each other. I wish I could do that too."

A humpback hug. I think that might have helped. "I wish you could too," I said.

She let out another long sound. And then everything went quiet again. I really needed to get home, to study for the debate, to get ready for something important, but I didn't. I stood there, pushing my feet into the pebbles on the beach.

"Life is meant to be and so is death," Meg said. "Just like

waves start, they crash. And death happens often in the ocean. But that doesn't mean that it doesn't hurt when it happens."

I mumbled my agreement and sat down just out of reach of the tide.

"I have children," Meg said. "They are grown and living their own lives now, but I can imagine what it would be like to lose someone that close to you. In fact, I can imagine very well."

I didn't know where this was going, but I waited. Maybe partly because I wanted to hear, and partly because the stings had frozen me. I didn't want to move. They could do that. Like when I didn't get out of bed for days.

"I can imagine it," Meg said, "because I've seen it. A gray whale I knew was expecting her first calf." Meg started into a story with a little less song. "She was so excited. It was her first. She sang about it all the time. I did that too when I was expecting. But with her, you could have known all about it for months and she'd still make it a point to tell you about it again. But when the cute gray whale calf was born, it didn't move." Meg paused. "It had died."

I gasped.

"The mother whale was devastated," Meg continued, "and in her sadness she lifted her child with her rostrum and carried that baby as her pod migrated. She carried it for days and days." I could picture it all in my head. "And when she got tired, others in her pod took over, carrying the baby, and giving it back to the mother when she wanted it back."

"Why?" I asked.

"She wasn't ready to let go," Meg said. "When something that sad happens, we don't usually move on very quickly."

I thought about that. "I know," I said, "but sometimes it would be nice if we could."

"Sure," Meg said, "but the more you love someone, the more it hurts when they're gone." Meg paused. "And that's okay."

I hugged my own knees. Meg was right. I loved my mom a whole lot. So it's not surprising that I miss her a whole lot too. That the pain is a whole lot.

"I wish—" Meg said, and then her call broke up a little. "I wish," she started again, "that I could carry your sadness a while for you."

I just sat there, hugging my knees tighter and pressing my feet in the pebbles. I did that for a while. What Meg had said sounded wonderful.

Finally, I spoke again. "For a little bit there," I said. "I think you kind of did." I took in a deep breath of ocean air. "Thanks."

And then it was like we both just appreciated one another. Like whatever space of ocean between us didn't matter. It felt like a humpback hug.

"I'm glad," Meg said. "And you're welcome. But the sorrow will come back over and over again."

"I know," I said, feeling it now and wondering when the next tsunami of sorrow would hit.

"You can talk with me whenever you need," Meg said.

That sounded perfect. "Thanks."

I sat there for just a few minutes more, then went home. I still had a debate to prepare.

CHAPTER 18

Debate

Willa Twitchell, Journal #5,
a week and a half ago

A while ago, I watched this video of a pod of orcas. They moved perfectly together. Like completely synchronized. You would have thought they were competing in the Olympics. In and out, they moved together, and although it was amazing, I couldn't help but feel like they were headed for trouble. Like the boys who roam the halls at school in a straight line so that nobody can pass by them. Or the girls who go to the dances in herds so that everyone else feels like a loser.

That's not entirely fair to orcas. They are hunters and always will be. It's like hating a grizzly bear because it's a grizzly bear, or a puma because it's a puma.

But I do have problems with those boys in the hall and those girls at the dances. I don't think they have to be that way.

"Okay," Mr. Norton said, "it's debate time."

Mr. Norton had Lizzy and Kaycen sit on one side of the front of the room while Jarom and I sat on the other.

I had to win this.

I had stayed up late trying to study, which was really hard with everything else going on in my mind. I couldn't stop thinking about Marc and the swim team. And my talk with Meg. But if I could beat Lizzy Wallace today, I would have at least something beautifully right in my life. Something worth celebrating.

"You remember the format," Mr. Norton said. "It's in your worksheets. Members of the team will alternate addressing us, then the structure will open up." He looked out at the class and then back at us. "The debate question was: Are video games and screens bad for children? Why don't we start with the affirmative team—saying screens are bad."

That was us.

I stood up and held my notebook. I didn't need it for notes or anything. I thought it made me look more prepared. "Study after study has shown that screen time, including video games, can cause problems with children. Lots of problems. For example, screens are addictive and could be just as addictive as chocolate, soda, and even drugs. When you play a video game or use social media, your brain releases a chemical called dopamine that makes you feel happy." I had looked up how to say that big word and practiced saying it out loud. I needed to sound smart. I thought it was working. "And that chemical makes you want more. Many people use their screens well past a normal amount of entertainment time. This reduces their normal social time with people in person and can create problems with their families, grades, and friends."

So far, so good. And it felt like my momentum was building. "And that's not all. Some studies show that violent video games can make people angry and aggressive. They can make people less likely to help other people out. They can make people more likely to be cruel and less likely to be kind." I raised my voice for effect. "I'm not making this up. I have my sources right here." I held up my notebook. I happened to glance at Marc. Instead of cheering me on, he sat slumped in his chair. He looked at me for a couple of seconds then looked away. Confused by his reaction, I stumbled over my words just a little. But then I got it back. "We need to turn off the screens, especially for children."

I finished my opening remarks almost as well as I had practiced in my room. Except for that little moment looking at Marc, I nailed it. Like really nailed it. I didn't want to get too confident, but that would be hard to beat.

Mr. Norton turned the time over to Lizzy.

She stood up and brushed off her dress. A dress. At school. She probably wore it just to look and feel more professional. It made her seem more like an adult. "Well," she started, "a lot of people think we should drastically reduce the time children spend on screens, particularly video games. And although we are not completely against reducing time, we would like to show you that completely turning off screens is no more realistic than the Luddites of the nineteenth century." She held her hands in front of her like a queen declaring her decision at a royal court. So formal. And completely ridiculous. I'm pretty sure none of us knew what Luddites were. And what did the nineteenth century have to do with screen time? The more she used words that nobody cared about, the easier it was going to be to win this debate.

"There are positive sides to screens," Lizzy said. "Spending a reasonable amount of time on screens and video games increases children's problem-solving and logic skills. It increases their hand-eye coordination, their fine motor and spatial skills. It teaches them perseverance, the value in taking risks, cooperation, and how to respond to challenges and frustrations. In fact, a study at Oxford University claimed that 'playing video games one hour a day actually enhanced psychological well-being in study participants.'" She paused to let that sink in. Then she curtsied like she was a princess at a ball. "Thank you."

What on earth? We weren't supposed to curtsy, were we? Who was she even thanking?

But her opening remarks were good. Really good. I wished they weren't, but they were. We needed to match them.

It was Jarom's turn to speak. He could respond to what Lizzy said and add new arguments. I looked over at him and I was pretty sure he hadn't been listening. I hoped he hadn't been playing a game on his phone while I had been trying to convince everyone to lower their screen time. Jarom's eyes went wide, then he fumbled through his folder. I'm not sure what took him so long. He only had three papers in that folder. The fact that I had to trust any of the debate to him drove me crazy. Finally, he stood up and cleared his throat. "We also looked at that Oxford study," he said. Good. He remembered. He was going to respond directly to something Lizzy had said. This was perfect. Jarom continued. "It also said that . . ." He searched his page for a moment. ". . . participants who played for over three hours a day had a decline in their well-being."

Solid. I had underestimated Jarom.

He gave a huge grin. "And we all heard what Willa said." Then he sat down.

I cringed. That was it? Of all the things we researched, that was it? He had shot too many lanky aliens and hadn't studied enough.

Kaycen then got to make a few points, which were decent. He talked about how games can give kids a sense of making their own choices and leading their own lives. Mr. Norton was making notes the whole time on the board and their side was getting bigger.

When Kaycen sat down, we were free to debate back and forth. We needed to gain back some ground. "Video games don't really give kids all of those positives," I said from my chair. "It's misleading. They only give kids the perception of them. It's make-believe. At the end of the day, what have they really accomplished?"

"This is all garbage," Derrin said from his seat. I guess I hurt his feelings about his screens. When I glanced at him, I also saw Marc, still slumped and grumpy.

Mr. Norton silenced Derrin. "It's not your debate."

Lizzy piped in. "A study in Norway showed that boys who spent time gaming didn't show any lack of social skills." Derrin whooped from his seat and some of the other kids joined him in cheering. Marc looked up.

What was going on here? Were they allowed to do that?

Kaycen followed. "In the right amounts, games and screen time can be healthy and good for your life."

There were more murmurs of agreement from the students in class.

Jarom held up a paper from his sloppy folder. "Well," he said reading it. "The *Journal of Psychology* said that screen time leads to impulserverty—"

"Impulsivity," I whispered.

"—and attention problems." He slammed the paper down on the table like he had just made a great point. I'm not sure he understood how to elaborate on a concept. One-sentence statements seemed to be all he could do.

"I would like to see the sources for that," Lizzy said, jumping to her feet and making her way to our table. Her dress swished as she walked. Jarom handed her the paper, pretty smugly. Especially since it was my research he was quoting. She scanned it for a moment. "That's what I thought," she said. "This is quoting a study done in 2012. Most research from that time period came to the same conclusion, but newer studies will show you that the old research was missing pieces of the puzzle. Were kids who played more video games becoming more impulsive—or were children with impulsive personalities drawn to video games?" She gave Jarom back his paper and went back to her table. "All of our research is from the last five years. Anything older than that is reactionary."

"Yeah!" Nolan shouted in agreement and everyone laughed. He never says words like impulsive or reactionary, even though he is both of those. He was just cheering for video games and we all knew it.

Lizzy and Kaycen went on to talk about studies that showed the educational value of screen time and video games—vocabulary, reading, math skills. How it introduces kids to tech and gets them interested in it. How it can increase some children's perseverance, memory, and concentration skills. In exact contrast to our points.

Jarom mentioned that kids who spent too much time on screens and playing video games were all fat. I knew what he was going for, but the way he said it wasn't true, especially since Jarom plays video games and definitely isn't fat. That got some boos from the class.

Mr. Norton asked them not to do that again, but the damage was done.

I talked about the dangers of children being online for games, especially social games, where there are bullies and predators. And I think the best piece I played was that the World Health Organization recognizes gaming addiction as a mental health disorder. "MRI scans reveal that addictive video games have a similar effect on the brain as drugs or alcohol. Plus, there is evidence that those who use too much screen time struggle in school."

I had their attention with that one.

When it was over Mr. Norton summarized all of the points on the board. The amount was pretty even on both sides. "Excellent job both groups. What a great way to start off our debates. Thanks for going first." That felt good, but I still wanted to beat Lizzy. I didn't know if he was going to grade us, or pronounce a winner or what.

Mr. Norton turned to the class. "Alright, this won't affect anyone's grades but out of curiosity, which side would you vote for?" A vote. This is how we would determine who was more persuasive.

He pointed at me and Jarom.

Only four hands went up.

My insides stormed. We were a total bomb.

Mr. Norton pointed to Lizzy's side and the rest of the hands in the room shot up. Everyone else. Even Jarom raised his hand until I swatted him in the stomach. Then he pulled it down. But one hand hurt the most. Marc's.

I felt betrayed. I mean, I knew he liked video games, but he could have pretended to vote for me just to be a friend.

Mr. Norton asked another question: "How many of you would have voted exactly the same as you did before the debate began?"

The hands all shot up. Every single person.

"Good to know," he said and dismissed us.

I had convinced nobody of anything. And Lizzy had beaten me, badly. Worse than in swim. Worse than in tests. She obliterated me.

I blinked hard as I shuffled all of my research into a tidy pile. And Marc didn't wait for me. There was no "that's too bad" or "good try." He was just gone. Then Lizzy was there, standing over me with a huge smug smile on her face. "Great job," she said, clearly pleased with herself. She put her hand out for a shake. But I didn't take it. It was no time for fake handshakes and smiles.

I hated everything.

CHAPTER 19

The Mendoza Marina

Willa Twitchell, Journal #5, today

<u>Eunice Aphroditois</u> sounds like a snobby girl. Like Aphrodite's less-pretty cousin. But really, it's the name of one of the most terrifying creatures in the ocean—the bobbit worm.

Imagine it. All you see is an inch or less of something poking out of the sand. Their iridescent skin even looks a little sparkly. Then when a fish swims by, not thinking much of the small, almost plant-like thing, it rockets out, snaps its scissor jaws, and pulls the stunned fish into the sand where it will be eaten. And it's strong. It can be several feet long under the ground, all of it pulling the fish in.

Terrifying.

Sometimes in life we think we know what's coming and then—<u>snap</u>!

I had to talk to Marc. I rode up to the Mendoza's house and when I reached the white fence around their front yard, I hopped off my bike. Yeah, it was one of those big red brick houses with a small white fence around it. Picture-perfect kind of thing. It was even on a hill with the ocean behind it. Seriously, it could be in movies.

I put my hand to the gate when a woman came out the front door. She had dark skin and her hair in a thick braid. A baby was perched on her hip and she shut the door behind her.

"Hello," she said as she walked right towards me. I guessed she had been visiting the Mendozas just before me. "I'm on my way out, but can I help you?"

Why would she help me? She was just visiting. Confused, I just said, "I'm looking for Marc."

She paused a moment, her mouth squishing to one side. Then her eyebrows lifted. "Mendoza?" she asked and adjusted the baby. "They don't live here anymore. We bought the house from them a few months ago." It all came rushing back. Jean had mentioned that Marc had moved. I felt stupid for not remembering it and not asking Marc more about it. "They had us forward their mail to their marina."

The marina? But I needed to know where he lived. Then again, the last few times we met up, I think Marc had come from the marina. Maybe he was there now.

I thanked the woman, jumped back on my bike, and shot down to the waterfront. As the marina came into view, it looked exactly how I remembered it, a large gray warehouse-looking building with a couple of huge garage doors and *Mendoza Marina* on a blue sign on top.

As I got closer, I could see Marc, his dad, and Dante, Marc's little brother, in the massive driveway wiping down a boat with rags. Marc's dad worked quickly, Marc regular speed, and Dante, Marc's six-year-old younger brother, did more flipping his towel than actually working.

When I pulled up, Marc's dad noticed me first. "I don't believe it," he said and set down his rag. "I haven't seen this *amiga* in years!" He made his way over to me. He had the same big smile as Marc. Well, the same smile Marc used to have. "Long time no see. Really long time." He looked down at himself. "I would hug you, but I'm a mess."

I just smiled. "It *has* been a long time. Good to see you, too."

"You should stay, hang out, have dinner with us," Marc's dad offered. That was classic Mendoza hospitality. Hello and invite to dinner. I had forgotten how great it was.

I looked at Marc. Did he want me to stay for dinner? He didn't give any hints. He focused on wiping down the boat. And he might have even been working a little faster than before.

"Yeah, stay for dinner," Dante said, taking the excuse to drop his rag.

"Do you remember Amiga?" Marc's dad said, pointing at me. I'm not sure he remembered my name, but I didn't mind "Amiga."

"No," Dante said. The kid was cute. "But Mama's making something super delicious." There was something about the way he spoke that I just loved. It was so perfect. I used to think that a child who was fluent in English and Spanish would have an accent, but he didn't. He switched from Spanish to English like it was nothing.

"What's she making?" I asked.

"I don't know," Dante said, "but it will be delicious. Unless it's mole sauce. That stuff is nasty." He stuck out his tongue.

"Dante," Marc's dad chided. Then he looked at me, "So . . . will you stay?"

I glanced at Marc again, but he still didn't look back. So I got bold. "What do you think, Marc?" I asked.

"Sure," he said, and gave a weak smile.

He definitely wasn't giving out an I-really-want-you-to-stay vibe, but I took the opportunity anyway. I texted my dad to ask permission, then picked up a towel from the stack on the ground and started helping. "So, I went to your old house . . ." I started. "I forgot you moved."

Marc winced.

"Where do you live now?" I asked.

"Oh, Amiga, Marc didn't tell you?" Marc's dad asked. "We moved here a few months ago. We converted part of the office into a little home for Maria and I, and the kids sleep out on our boat." He pointed with his towel hand to the office in the back, then to their sailboat that was rocking against the dock. "It's just for now while we look for a new place."

"Oh, okay," I said. I hadn't realized they were living at the marina. And now that I thought about it, Marc seemed like he didn't want me to know that. Was he embarrassed to be sleeping in a boat while they looked for a new house? I didn't understand that. It might be fun to sleep in a boat, being rocked to sleep.

"But you're going to buy a new place on the island, right? You're not moving far?"

"My work is here," Marc's dad said with his arms outstretched. "We won't go far."

"Good," I said, trying to figure out what to do with the wet towel I was holding. I twisted some water out of it and moved closer to Marc and Dante. "Why didn't you tell me any of this?" I asked Marc.

He shrugged, then looked at his brother.

"Hey, Dante," Marc said, "you're supposed to be washing the boat, not the entire driveway around it." He always teased his brother, but I got the feeling he was trying to change the subject.

Dante just looked up. "Burn," he said.

Marc smiled wide and looked at me. I think he was expecting that answer.

"I don't think you usually say burn," I explained, "if someone says something mean to you. Just if they say it to someone else."

"Burn again," Dante said.

Marc and I full-on laughed. Dante really didn't understand. We wiped the boat and then Mr. Mendoza used his truck to pull it into the dockyard, just in time for Marc's mom to call us all in for dinner.

As we came into a little kitchen just off the office, Mamá Mendoza kissed everyone on the forehead, even me. Especially me. "Good to have you here, Willa. You are getting prettier all the time." She hugged me.

At home, I felt like one more thing to stress Masha out. Here

I was invited, kissed, and hugged. I was wanted. Except maybe not by Marc. He was still being a little weird.

The room felt warm from all of the cooking, and a spicy smell filled the air. Mamá Mendoza pulled a pot of boiled chicken and rice off the stovetop and placed the sizzling food in front of us.

We dug in. Mamá Mendoza's food was always yummy. Papá Mendoza was also a talented cook, but Mamá was the best.

"This is great," I said between bites of chicken. It was seriously good. Soon we launched into conversation about school and video games and how exactly Dante had spilled the lemonade on the Xbox. Marc even smiled a few more times. And everything felt right somehow.

Wait. Not everything.

Something was off. Not with the food. Something else. Even with all the talk, the table was quieter. No, not quieter, just— Sofia, Marc's sister. She wasn't here.

"Where's Sofia?" I asked.

For a split second, everything paused.

"She's away for a little while," Marc's dad said, and everyone went back to eating. Even Dante focused on the plate in front of him. Suddenly, everything felt awkward.

Mamá Mendoza put down her fork and looked at me. She tilted her head and tried to explain. "She's at a hospital in Everett."

"For schooling." Papá Mendoza piped in. "She's learning lots." He took a big bite of food.

"Oh," I said, "that's cool. What's she studying?"

"Health," Papá Mendoza said and smiled, but it was different.

In fact, it reminded me of some faces Marc had made recently. A little fake and angry. Or something just a little off.

"Will she be back for summer?" I asked.

Marc's mom shook her head.

"Probably longer," Dante said, obviously repeating what his parents had told him.

"Yeah," Marc's dad said, "we don't know for sure. She has to finish what she's doing. She's really busy and it's really important. Hopefully she comes back soon, though." And he smiled the same way as before. I didn't understand that. Why would a smile be fake when his daughter was off at school?

I looked at Marc, but he didn't look back. He just kept eating, his left hand clenched into a fist. Was this what they were spending money on? Was her schooling so expensive that Marc couldn't join the swim team?

Something felt off. Sofia didn't seem like the type to work in a hospital. She was nice and everything, but not that focused—she was more fun-loving and impatient. I could picture all of the other Mendozas working in a hospital before I could picture Sofia. Had she changed that much since I had last been here? But then, why all the awkwardness about it?

"Can you name ten Pokémon?" Dante asked out of nowhere. "Because I can name like 700."

"Oh, no," Marc said, his fist unclenching a little. "Just don't ask him to do it." He shook his head a couple of times. "He'll go on for hours." I could imagine that and how much it would bother Marc. His parents seemed to agree.

"I can't name any," I said, though I might be able to name a couple. "Can you name ten different types of whales?"

Dante thought for a moment. "Gray, blue, black, white . . ."

Marc raised his hand between bites of chicken. "Don't ask Willa how many she can name, either. She can go on for hours too."

I couldn't help but push him a little, which almost made him spit out his chicken. Which made everyone laugh.

I was so glad I came. We talked and ate and talked. And after we all finished, I told them that I'd better get going. I hoped Marc would see me out so I could make sure he was okay.

"Thank you so much for coming," Mamá Mendoza said. "Come back any time."

"It was good to see you," Papá Mendoza said.

"Yes," Dante said. Was he saying it was good to see me too? "But next time know some Pokémon." He paused. "Burn."

Maybe he was catching on. I loved that kid.

I said thank you and Marc followed me out.

There was a storm starting, I could tell. There was something about the taste to the air. I'd better get on my bike soon. "Thanks for letting me come over," I said as we walked toward my bike under a big fir tree.

"I didn't really get to choose," he said, looking at the sky. The clouds moving in were darker.

I wasn't sure if that was a joke or if he was upset. I thought dinner went well and he was happier. Maybe not.

"Sorry." I didn't mean to make him feel like I was pushing my friendship on him. The whole reason I had come was to make sure he was okay. He had kind of freaked out after swim, and then he didn't even talk to me after the debate. "Are you okay? Things got a little awkward when we talked about Sofia."

He looked at me. "Yeah," he said, "I am a little upset that . . . well, Sofia . . ." He wasn't making sense. He clenched his fist again. "It's personal stuff."

I nodded. He didn't have to tell me anything. But I wished he would. I had always liked Sofia. She was three years older than us and always made me laugh and Marc blush. Maybe he just really missed her. Or maybe he was mad that her schooling cost so much.

"I've been thinking about it," I said, "and I'd like to pay for you to do swim with me. I got some inheritance money—"

"Stop it!" He cut me off.

I jumped. I hadn't seen that coming.

"I *don't* want you to pay for me and I *don't* want you to bring it up again." His musselcracker face was back.

I just stared at him. He had full-on yelled at me.

"I'm just trying to help," I defended.

"But you're not," he said. "Just don't."

"But do you need me to—"

"Just don't," he cut me off again, his voice just as loud. I expected his mom or dad to come running out the door to see what had their son all riled up. I wanted them to come. Maybe then Marc would calm down.

But no one opened the door. I stood under a tree, getting drizzled on through the branches and listening to my only friend yell at me for trying to help him.

Marc spoke again. "Just leave me alone."

And then the closest thing I had to a friend turned and walked back into the marina office and slammed the door.

CHAPTER 20

The Shadow

Willa Twitchell, Journal #5, today

A big storm hit last night. Some kids my age still get scared when storms roll in. They are pretty dangerous on our island. But I get really excited. The louder and windier, the better. Because that means cool stuff washes up.

My mom and I always rushed down to the beach the first thing in the morning after a storm. Once I found a Pacific spiny lumpsucker in the tide pool. A cute green one with big blue eyes that looked like sapphires and a tiny, darling mouth. It was shaped like a ball and had suction cup feet on the bottom. I wanted to take him home so bad, but I knew he needed to stay in the ocean. My mom was impressed. She said the bright green color meant that he was far from home.

I like storms because of what they wash in. But

then I started to worry about that tiny, quarter-sized fish. I hoped it could find its way home. Swim, lump-sucker! You can do it!

~~~~~~~~~~~~~~~~~~~~~~~~~~~~~~~~~~

I was up at 5:30, threw my hair in a ponytail, didn't even brush it, and threw on a hoodie. This early on the northwest coast was cold, even in the spring.

The morning after a storm.

Well, actually it was the morning after two storms—one in the sky and one in me. I couldn't stop thinking about how badly last night ended with Marc. I messed everything up. I didn't really know what I did wrong or how to fix it.

Nothing was going right, not getting a friend, not debate, nothing. Tide pools might help me think. Or at least distract me.

After a storm, the most interesting things wash ashore. My mom had an entire collection of Japanese glass fishing balls that she'd collected on Tupkuk Island after storms. I only found one with her. Not many washed up anymore, but I always crossed my fingers that I would find another.

I have found a seahorse not native to Washington, wolf eels, a big starfish with ten legs, and a broken wooden chest. I like to think it used to be pirate property, but missing the treasure.

I hoped I'd find something today.

I left a note for my dad and took off for the beach. I was getting faster on my bike from exercising for swim, but now it probably didn't matter.

"Glad you're back," Meg said after I called her. Apparently, humpback whales don't sleep in either. "I've thought of a lot of questions I really want to ask a human. Like how can you possibly stand upright? Why do you eat so many different things? And what's it like to have both your eyes on the front of your face instead of on the sides of your head like me? How can you see a shark coming behind you?"

The questions took me off guard. "I can answer those later, Meg," I said, scanning the shore for anything new or out of place.

"Are you feeling okay?" Meg asked. Immediately I remembered how I told her about my mom. I didn't regret it. That was one thing that had actually been good in the last few days.

"I'm okay," I said. But just because I talked about my mom last time, didn't mean I wanted to talk about her now. Under some seaweed, I found an orange longfin sculpin, not the brown ones I usually saw. I pulled my phone out of my pocket.

"Meg, what do you do if someone is mad at you and you're not exactly sure why?"

"Hmmm, that sounds like a difficult situation," she sang.

"It is." I got pictures of the sculpin.

"Well," she said, "there is a legend that a small pod of beluga whales were stolen from their homes in the arctic, and were brought to work for the humans as spies."

I wasn't really sure what this had to do with my question, but she had my attention.

"They called these belugas the Cold Ops," Meg explained. "I never met a Cold Op myself, but plenty of whales that I trust have told me about meeting them where the water starts turning warm. Anyway, one of these Cold Ops was named No-Sea, clearly named by people, because that makes a terrible call. But it is said that No-Sea learned to talk to people. Not like how I speak to you. No-Sea could speak to *all* people. He wasn't supposed to be able to speak human but he did . . ." She was quiet like she was thinking. "Where was I going with this?"

"That I should get a whale to spy on my friend to find out why he's angry?" I asked.

"Oh, no," Meg said. "I was just thinking that if No-Sea and humans can talk, and if you and I can talk, maybe you and your friend could talk. He could tell you himself. That would be better than any spy."

I thought about that for a moment. "That sounds good," I said, "but what if the person doesn't want to talk?"

"You've got a silent clam, do you?" Meg said. "Well, make sure that they know that you are always willing to talk to them even if they're not ready to talk to you." That sounded like something my mom would say.

I had spent the night missing my mom, thinking about Marc, and wishing I knew how to help him. I wished he'd just let me pay for swim team.

I had walked a good portion of the tide pools and hadn't been looking as hard as I should have. I stepped down from the rocks and onto the pebble beach when I noticed something large on the far end of the beach, just barely in the break.

"What is that?" I said, mostly to myself.

"Are you pointing?" Meg asked. "You need to remember that I can't see you."

"There's a boat, I think," I said. "Down a ways on the shore.

Tipped over." But I had never seen a boat here. Maybe it was washed in from the storm.

I started walking towards it. With the sun rising behind it, it left a silhouette, like a shadow, hard to identify. "I'm going to check it out."

"Are you sure it looks like a boat?" Meg asked. There was a tenseness to her voice I didn't understand.

"Yeah," I said. "Well, I don't know what else it would be." I couldn't really tell. "I'm coming up on it." And right as I said that I noticed that it looked odd. It wasn't exactly the size of a boat. More . . . floppy. And something was sticking out of the side. Like a sail? Nope. Like a fin. My heart stopped, then crashed down through my chest.

"It's a whale," I said in total unbelief, and then sprinted toward the poor thing.

"Oh, no," Meg said.

The closer I got to it, the bigger it got. And bigger. And bigger. It was absolutely huge. "It's bigger than you," I said quietly. "A lot bigger."

"Bigger than me?" Meg said with the same quiet awe. "Is it moving?"

I searched the thing with my eyes as best I could. I scanned from mouth to tail for any sign of movement. Then right as I opened my mouth to answer, a soft breath escaped from its blowhole. "It's alive."

Meg let out a series of calls.

Cautiously, I got closer. It was the size of an eight-story building lying on its side. Seriously huge. I felt tiny next to it. "Hello?"

I said to the whale, but it didn't respond. I didn't even know if I could talk to any other whales, but I had to try.

"It's a blue." As the words slid out, it all felt surreal. I had always wanted to see a blue whale. Larger than the dinosaurs. A true behemoth of this world. "It's a blue whale," I repeated to Meg. One of the most majestic creatures ever. A total titan. Stuck on *my* beach. This was not how I wanted to see one in person for the first time.

"Take a deep breath," Meg said. I guess she could hear how tense I was. "There is a pod of blue whales near here. I'll reach out to them."

"Can you talk to it?" I asked. "I can't but maybe you can."

"I already tried, dear. It must be too exhausted," Meg said. "Now listen to me." She sounded serious. "Being stuck on land is a whale's worst nightmare. I wish I could come up on the shore and help, but I can't. I need you to do it. Please do everything you can."

"I will," I said, but the whale looked so still.

A stillness like I'd seen a little over a month ago.

A stillness I never wanted to see again.

CHAPTER 21

911

Willa Twitchell, Journal #5, today

Blue whales are the largest creatures in the world. They are as big as three school buses put together. But it would be so much cooler to ride a blue whale than a bus. Of course, I'm assuming I had scuba gear and a way to hold on.

Blue whales grow so big because gravity doesn't affect creatures as much under water. There is no way a whale could grow so huge if it had to walk around on land. Blue whales are also one of the loudest animals. Its calls can get as high as 188 decibels. That's louder than a rock concert.

Did you know that you can figure out how old a blue whale is by the amount of earwax it has? I know. Gross. But still, that's cool and super interesting. They get another layer of wax every six months, so you can count them like rings on a tree. The oldest one ever found was 110 years old. That's great-great-grandma blue whale. And a blue whale eats four tons of food a day. That's four times what a human eats in a whole year.

But when I finally met one in person, I really wished it could have been in totally different circumstances.

"911. What's your emergency?" the operator asked. She sounded professional but concerned.

"I need help," I said, finally freeing my arm from my hoodie and removing it. I had to be careful not to drop my phone or get it too wet, but this whale needed me.

I had never called 911 before. My pulse rolled and crashed like waves against the rocks. "I'm at Rocky Cove Beach, on the south end." I was in the tide mid-shin, my hoodie in my hand. The whale hadn't moved at all and its eyes were closed. I thought that was good. When things die they often have their eyes open, right? Hopefully it was just resting.

My first instinct was to push it back into the water. I know: that's incredibly stupid. It weighs tons and tons. I weigh eighty-seven pounds. It would be like me pushing a semitruck with two full trailers. Scratch that—it would be like me pushing a house, maybe even a couple of houses.

Nope. Definitely not.

I needed better ideas.

Like calling the authorities.

Thinking about how much the whale weighed made me even

more nervous. I was on the lookout for any movement. Even a tail swish could do some serious damage to little me. That thing had muscles bigger than my whole body.

And its skin was still slick and wet. That was good. It hadn't dried out.

"What's the emergency?" the lady asked for clarification.

"There's a beached whale," I blurted out, while dunking my hoodie in the water. "It needs help fast." I took my wet hoodie and put it on the side of its face. I had to keep it wet. And once placed I realized that one hoodie was impressively insufficient, like hardly did anything.

A bucket and towels would be really useful about now.

Scratch that. About a hundred buckets and towels and a hundred other people. Hopefully the authorities would bring them.

"Did you say a beached whale?" the operator asked.

"Yes," I said. "Rocky Cove Beach. South end. You have to go across the highway by Dahl Road, then go down the steep trail. But I need help fast."

There was an uncomfortable pause on the other end of the line. I kicked water up at the whale because I was afraid of it getting dry. Like the hoodie, it wasn't going to be enough to change anything, but I had to try. And even a little had to help, right? But I was careful to avoid the blowhole. If water got in the blowhole, it would be like us getting water in our lungs. And the last thing I needed to do would be choke a stranded whale. "We need to get it help fast," I repeated.

Still nothing.

"Hello? I said there's a beached whale here," I repeated.

Another pause. "I'm sorry, but we don't handle beached whales," she said. "I'm trying to find someone who can help you."

What? 911 was for emergencies. That's why they exist. What did she mean that she didn't handle them? This was a huge emergency. Like biggest-creature-on-earth huge. I pulled my hoodie off the whale and got it wet again.

I stood there, holding the hoodie, not sure where to put it to do the most good. Not sure that I was doing any good at all, I felt afraid I was going to start crying from being overwhelmed.

"I'm back." The lady on the phone startled me. "I have a phone number for the Marine Mammal Stranding Hotline. Would you like me to connect you?"

Her voice snapped me back into action. I picked a spot and placed the hoodie. "Yes, please."

It was quiet again while she connected the call.

The whale hadn't breathed again, or maybe it had and I was just too stressed out to notice. I put my ear to its body, hoping to hear a heartbeat. A blue whale's heart only beats like ten times a minute, so I'd have to be patient. The heart was the size of a car and its arteries were so big, a kid a little smaller than me could probably swim through them.

I listened but heard nothing.

When a blue whale's heart beats in the ocean, you can hear it up to two miles away. But I couldn't hear anything now.

Come on. Come on. Come on.

I tried to stop myself, but I couldn't help but think of my mom and her heart. Had something like that happened to this whale?

"It's okay," I said to the whale, "we're getting help." I hoped that maybe, just maybe, it could understand me like Meg.

But nothing.

I waited on the phone, listening for the operator, or the heartbeat, or the whale to respond, whichever came first. Every second dragged at seahorse speed.

"Hello, this is Charles at the Granata Island Observation Station." Someone had finally answered. I rattled off the details about the whale and how it was stuck and needed help now. "We'll be there as soon as we can," he said. And he sounded like he was grabbing things. I even heard him call out to someone else at the station. Finally—someone who treated this like an emergency.

"Thank you," I said.

"Please don't go near the animal," he said.

"Okay," I lied. It was too late for that. And Charles hung up.

Someone was coming. Someone who knew how to help. I kicked more water on Blue. I guess I had named him Blue in my mind. Suddenly it registered that Charles said he was from Granata Island. That wasn't very close. He'd have to take a ferry to get here.

That left me alone, kicking insignificant amounts of water up on a giant blue whale for a long time.

CHAPTER 22

Help

Willa Twitchell, Journal #5, today

No one really knows why whales get beached, but we have some guesses. Sometimes they were dead before and float up onto shore. Sometimes they get sick and disoriented. Also, the sonar we use in boats might mess up their echolocation or their brain waves. And there is another reason, and it terrifies me.

"Meg?" I called out.

She didn't answer. I waited and she still didn't answer. There wasn't much she would be able to do from the middle of the ocean but I needed help, I needed someone.

I called my dad. He didn't answer either. He kept his phone off in the mornings sometimes. I left a message telling him that I needed his help, then called the only other person I could think of. After our earlier conversation, I wondered if he'd pick up.

He didn't.

It was early, like 6:30. He probably wasn't even awake yet.

I didn't know who else to call, so I tried again. As I pressed the buttons on my phone, I worried that I must seem obnoxious, calling him twice in a row like this, plus waking him so early. It might just make him angrier.

But I had to do something.

It rang three times.

"Hey, Willa," Marc said, answering this time, half yawning. But he didn't sound upset, so that was good. And the fact that he picked up was all that mattered right now.

"Can you get to our beach, now?" I frantically asked. "There's this stranded whale and it's stuck and I'm really scared that it's going to die if we don't help it."

"What?" His voice rose in confusion.

"I need help now," I repeated. "A beached whale. I'm afraid it's going to . . ." Tears streamed down my face. "Oh. Just hurry." I couldn't form my sentences very well. My mind was like a typhoon of terror and nerves.

"Okay okay okay," he said superfast, one word bleeding into the next. "I'm coming. Are you at our normal spot?"

"No," I said. "Well, close. Just down the shore towards downtown. You'll see us."

I heard him calling out something loud in Spanish to his family. Was he waking them up? I couldn't tell what he said but he was probably telling them why he had to go somewhere this early.

I wished he were here. Stat.

"We need all the blankets or towels that we can get wet," I said. "Buckets too, maybe shovels . . ." My brain couldn't think past the obvious.

"Is it alive?" he asked. I could hear him breathing hard as if he was running around.

"I think so," I said, though I was getting nervous since I hadn't heard the heart and it had been a bit since it breathed. "Please hurry."

My eyes wanted to cry, but I wouldn't let them.

"I'm leaving right now," Marc said and hung up.

People were coming. Charles and Marc.

I wasn't going to have to do this by myself.

There was so much relief in that idea. But there was still a lot to do if we were going to save this whale. What would my mom do if she were here?

It hurt to think about her, but I had to. What would she do? What would she do? What?

Keep the skin moist. I was trying.

Notify authorities. I'd done that.

Keep the environment calm. Check.

Now what?

I kicked water up on Blue again and again, now just trying to keep myself from crying. I tried my dad again, but he didn't answer.

I kicked some more. Once a wave hit me from behind and almost knocked me over. It soaked me through.

But that was good.

It also hit Blue.

A big wave like that also meant the tide was rising, which would make it easier for us to get the whale back out to sea.

In and out, the water surrounded the massive body, and then it pulled out, sucking around the pebbles as it left.

I imagined what it must be like to live your entire life in the buoyancy of the salt water and then find yourself, all tons and tons of you, stuck out in the dry air, with all of the gravity that comes with it. The weight on his body must have been huge.

Hurry, rescue crew. Hurry.

I still hadn't heard the whale breathe. But blue whales could go over an hour without breathing, swimming for long periods underwater. So he might still be okay.

Walking around him, I tried to determine if he was injured or struggling.

I passed the baleen, the whale's filter and feeding system—like a giant drain in its mouth. Baleen whales never attacked large prey, let alone humans—they didn't have the teeth to eat them. But I still didn't get that close. It's not wise to tempt a scared animal with a monstrous mouth.

Chills ran through me as I studied this mammoth beast in the shadowy morning light all by myself.

Its eyes were so tiny compared to how big the whole creature was. So tiny, the size of baseballs. And closed.

Don't be dead.

Don't be dead.

I don't need any more dead in my life.

The largest animal ever to live on our planet—larger than

even the biggest dinosaurs. One of the least understood animals in the entire ocean. Just lying on my beach. In my cove. Maybe dying.

I needed help—soon.

I reached the tail, and from what I could see everything looked okay. No obvious injuries. But I couldn't really see the top of the whale because it was too high for me and I couldn't see its underside.

I splashed water up on the back of Blue and worked my way to the front. I carefully continued to use my hoodie to try to keep it wet without getting water in the blowhole.

It wasn't enough.

But I didn't know anything else to do.

I did it again and again.

Ten minutes.

Twenty minutes.

I'm not even sure how long it had been, but my arms and legs were sore and my spirits low. I was draining fast.

Still it didn't breathe.

But that was okay, right? It hadn't been an hour.

I kicked hard at the water to splash lots of it across Blue's tail. I wasn't sure how much longer I could go.

"Willa."

Finally.

It was Marc. He had beat the emergency people.

And there were people behind him.

"Sorry, Willa," he said. "We came as fast as we could."

We—he said *we*. My heart almost burst. Not just a little help.

Behind Marc was his dad, his mom, and Dante. They paused at the top of the rocks and Papá Mendoza whistled.

"Oh, Amiga." He held ropes and a shovel. "This is huge."

"Wow." Dante almost exhaled the word. He was still in his Pokémon pajamas.

"*Wow* is right," a voice said from behind them.

It was my dad.

He got my message.

CHAPTER 23

The Plan

Willa Twitchell, Journal #5, today

Blue whales have the biggest hearts on the planet. They can pump fifty-eight gallons with every beat. My heart is about the size of my dad's fist and pumps a couple ounces with each beat.

I just really wanted everyone's hearts: mine, blue whales', everyone's and everything's to just keep beating.

~~~~~~~~~~~~~~~~

The Mendozas brought with them buckets and towels, just like I asked. The boys went to work right away gathering water and keeping the whale wet.

Marc's parents and my dad walked around the whale with me as I tried to explain when I found it and what little I'd already done. "I thought this was going to be a lot smaller whale," Marc's dad said. He held up his rope and shovel. "This isn't going to do any good."

"We can't push it back out," my dad said as we came back to Blue's head. "Not with a hundred people."

I felt helpless not knowing what to do. Usually I was so good with my oceanic knowledge but this one stumped me. I knew stories of whale strandings. I knew stories where fifty people were able to push a stranded whale back to sea. But that was with a lot smaller whales. Online, I had seen large cranes lift whales back out to deeper water. But those were smaller whales too. I had seen strandings where they put the whale in a harness and pulled it out to sea with a boat. I had seen people dig around the whale so that the sand gave out beneath it and it could float in the water and swim away. I had seen them nurture stranded whales until the tide rose again and they were free.

None of those whales were this big.

Not even close.

The ones that I knew of were baby humpbacks, or sperm whales, or belugas. This thing was a titan compared to those.

"We need more people," Mamá Mendoza said. "More than a hundred. A thousand. Two thousand. We should get the whole island out here. Then we might be able to move it." She would do it, too.

"It's too heavy," Marc's dad said to his wife. "I have my boat and tow chains, but it would take a whole fleet to move this thing."

"Even if that would work, the water is too shallow and too rocky here," my dad said. "You couldn't get within seventy-five

yards of this whale with a boat. But I don't have any better ideas."
He scratched the back of his head. "Poor thing doesn't look good."

"Please step away from the whale," a voice from a megaphone
said.

I looked over my shoulder and saw two silhouettes approaching.

"We need help," I said. "We're trying to get this whale back
into the water."

"Please just step away," the man said again coming closer into
view. "Whales like this can be very dangerous."

"Dangerous?" Mamá Mendoza said, and then let out a stream
of Spanish that I couldn't understand. I'm guessing she was calling her kids back.

"Is one of you Willa?" the other person said. This one was a
woman and didn't have a megaphone.

I raised my hand. "Are you guys from the Granata Island
Observation Station?"

The man nodded. "Charles and Clarissa Goodwin." He
waved an introduction. I couldn't see their faces very well, but he
was as round as a teddy bear.

The woman was tall and skinny. "You did the right thing
in calling us." She pointed toward the top of the whale's head.
"Charles, look." She let out a sigh.

I followed her finger. I still couldn't see the top of the whale's
head, but there was a dark line that looked like it was dripping
down the side of its head. It was in the shadow and very thin. I
could see how I missed it, but I felt really dumb. I hoped it didn't
mean what I thought it meant.

"Did you touch it at all?" she asked looking at me, then my dad and the Mendozas.

"Yes," I admitted.

"Be sure to wash yourselves very, very well when you get home," Clarissa explained. "Beached creatures can carry diseases."

"Can we save it?" Papá Mendoza asked. "I can call my friends and get boats and tow ropes if any of that would be helpful. But I don't know, it's so big . . ."

"No," Charles said, using a flashlight to get a good look at the head. "That can actually be really dangerous for the animal. We use specialized equipment to tow a whale. And this guy would need a lot of it. But thank you for offering."

Papá Mendoza nodded.

Clarissa put on some plastic gloves, approached the whale's eye, and lifted the lid.

I cringed, waiting for the whale to respond. I know if someone did that to me while I was sleeping, I would hit them pretty hard. I wouldn't mean to. Just a reaction.

But then she did something that would freak me out even more. She pressed a few fingers against the eye. Yep. Right on the eye. That couldn't feel good.

But the whale didn't move. Poor thing must have been in really bad shape, in a total daze.

Charlie started jotting notes on a small notepad he pulled out of his pocket.

"He's a blue whale," Clarissa said.

I pointed to the tail. "And he has some identifying markings on the fluke." I pinched my mouth shut. I was just trying to be helpful but feared I might have sounded a little smart-mouthed.

"Wow," Charles said going to check out the tail. "You talk like a pro."

My cheeks grew warm and I grinned. "My mom is a marine biologist."

"Here on Tupkuk?" Charles asked, examining the tail markings.

"She used to be." It felt strange to suddenly be making small talk. We had a huge titan of a whale that needed us. And even under the circumstances, I felt another sting. Mom would know better what to do than me.

"What's her name?" Clarissa asked, joining Charles to look at the tail. Why were they so calm?

I took a deep breath, the kind a whale probably takes when it's going to be underwater for the next forty-five minutes. But I let mine out. "Maylan Twitchell," I said.

There was a moment of recognition, and then they both looked at each other. "Oh," Clarissa said, "we're so sorry. I loved your mom."

I smiled, but it was hollow. I loved her more. It was still good to hear that people knew her and loved her too. But she would want us to help this whale.

Charles crouched, and he and Clarissa spoke to each other. Then he stood up. "Thank you so much for your help," he said. "You did a wonderful job. You can feel free to go home. We'll take it from here."

"What about the whale?" Mamá Mendoza asked, Dante standing beside her.

"We will discuss this with our greater team and decide what to do tomorrow," Clarissa explained.

"We can't just wait until tomorrow," I said. "We have to do something. We have to save it."

"For your safety, and because of protocol, you're going to have to leave now," Charles said, scrunching up his face like he didn't like it either.

"I don't want to leave," I said. "I want to help. We have to get this whale back out in the water. Or we have to put more water on him. Something."

Clarissa walked over to me. "I'm sorry, Willa." She took a deep breath. "But the whale is dead."

I blinked, trying to process what she said. I ran that word through my head again.

"It didn't look alive when we came, but pressing against its eye was a test. It didn't respond." She waited a moment. "I'm sorry."

Dead? Somewhere in me, I had known, but I'd hoped it away.

This huge beautiful blue whale wasn't alive. I shook my head. All of my work wasn't enough.

"I'm sorry," she repeated. "And we will take it from here. Thank you so much for your help."

I fell to the beach. I think my legs turned to squid tentacles. And my tears drained out. I had seen one of the biggest, most magnificent creatures in the world. I had touched it. I was in the right place to help. And I failed.

Maybe a whale out there had just lost their dad or brother or friend because I wasn't good enough.

CHAPTER 24

A Haze

Willa Twitchell, Journal #5, today

That was the second time I've been there when the world lost one of its best.

Blue whales are one of the absolutely most epic creatures in the history of time. But even though they're enormous, in the 332.5 million cubic miles of water in the ocean, rarely does anyone see one. And they are endangered. Rare and endangered.

My mom was about seventy-five feet shorter than a blue whale and sixty-five and nineteen-twentieth tons less. But she was even more rare. And to be honest, about a duodecillion tons awesomer. And miles and miles more important. And she left a blue whale–sized hole in my world.

Why did she have to go?

And why does this keep happening to me?

In a haze, I looked out over the beach where Blue was. Blue. It was a good name for a good whale.

The ocean still curled in waves and lapped, but it didn't calm me. The in and out was almost annoying. Those waves had brought Blue in and then we lost him.

Lost him.

I hated that phrase. We didn't *lose* him. He was right there. When people would say that it was so sad that I lost my mom, I bristled. I didn't lose her. She wasn't a misplaced shoe. She was dead, not lost. And it made it sound like I had some responsibility in it, like I had absentmindedly left her someplace.

"I'm sorry," Dante said, and gave me a hug while I still sat on the sand. Sweet. But I didn't hug him back. I wasn't all there. My mind was replaying any mistakes I might have made.

The titan was dead. Blue was gone.

It didn't work. I called the experts, I called in my friends, I tried to keep him wet, and it still didn't work.

It was like my personal ocean was filled with a bloom of jelly-fish and their stings. They were everywhere. I couldn't swim a stroke without another stab of pain.

So I didn't try to swim. I didn't try to move.

It hurt too much.

I think a few more people spoke, but I was somewhere in a fog. My eyes glossed over and my mind reeled.

Dead.

More words around me. Marc? But I didn't move. The amazing whale had been right here and now part of him was gone.

Gone somewhere else. And the whale probably had a son or daughter out there that was about to get the absolute worst news of their lives. Or worse yet, maybe they would swim around, wandering aimlessly looking for their father or friend and hoping he would be just around the next reef, or just out of sight in the darkness beneath them, or a shadow about to swim over them.

And once they really knew, once it settled in, they would try to move on, but they would still pass spots where he used to be and wonder. And miss. And feel weak, like the current just got ten times harder to swim against.

And maybe they wouldn't feel like swimming at all. Not alone. Maybe they would just hover there, not even knowing where to go, letting the current pull them wherever it wanted.

And maybe in an ocean of sixty million square miles with over 200,000 different kinds of creatures swimming and living and growing around them, they would suddenly feel completely alone.

Like me.

Right then in my life, it felt like there might be more jellyfish than water to swim in.

Dad pulled me to my feet and wrapped his arms around me. I felt his beard on my forehead. He was in his suit coat, ready to leave for work. And because he was hanging around the ocean with me, he smelled like sea rock—earthy but salty—and fish. He'd probably ruined his suit. For me.

I think he said something, maybe thanking Charles, Clarissa, and the others and I let him scoop me up and carry me up the trail. That had to be hard, but I didn't realize it at the time.

Eventually, my dad set me down on the seat of his truck.

Again voices. Mamá Mendoza. Then Marc. But I couldn't focus on any words.

The car started up. My dad was looking forward as he pulled off the crunchy gravel onto the highway.

"I'm really sorry, sweetheart," he said.

Part of me wanted to say something, but I wasn't going to be able to make sentences. At least not ones that made sense. At least not without dissolving into a puddle of tears.

But the tears came anyway.

They came for the whale and his family.

They came for a life that was gone and all the hollow that would come. But mostly they came for me.

For my mom.

"Just know that whenever you want to talk," he said. "I'm ready to listen."

I wanted to talk. I was going to have to talk. I opened my mouth hoping something would come. Something that would make sense. Something that would pull me out of this mass of emotion. A whale's weight of feelings.

Zero percent chance. So I closed it again.

I did want to talk.

Desperately.

But when and how, I couldn't figure out.

Not now. Not here.

But soon.

Before I exploded.

CHAPTER 25

Tell Them

Willa Twitchell, Journal #5, yesterday

I couldn't go to school. Not now. And my dad didn't make me.

Blue whales were put on the endangered species list before my parents were born, like 1967. At one time, there were hundreds of thousands of them. But they were hunted and now they're one of the rarest whales. Researchers estimate there are 10,000 to 25,000 of them left in all the world. That's not a lot compared to over seven billion people, or like 900 million dogs. They are still endangered and very slowly recovering.

I really, really, really, really wished I could have saved this one.

5:30 A.M.

And I was awake. Just like yesterday.

I rolled over and remembered everything. Both the whale and Mom.

That had happened yesterday. I didn't go to school, or to swim practice. Which didn't really matter because Marc wasn't going either. I didn't leave my room. I rolled over again and again, thinking everything over and over and inside-out and through. I wanted to cry, to punch something, and scream. I wanted to be in the ocean, just floating there. Just being. Just away from here.

A million stings.

But this morning was slightly better. I had only rolled over about 287 times since waking up. 7:00 A.M. came and went. I didn't even try to get up for school. In the back of my mind I thought of Marc. I needed to thank him and his family. He had texted a few times yesterday, but I didn't respond. I didn't know what to say. I still didn't know what he was being all upset and secretive about, but he had come when I needed him.

But that was in the back of my mind. The rest of my mind stormed. I'm not even sure it was really thinking, just soaking me, drenching me, drowning me. It was like I was on a sinking skiff out on the ocean during a hurricane. I could try to sail out of there. I could try to stay dry. I could lift my fists to the heavens and curse them, but none of it would do any good.

So I didn't move.

And Dad didn't wake me. From inside the storm I liked that. He had already given me one day off. He could have insisted I wake up and go to school today. But he didn't. Maybe he knew I was in a storm. A storm I couldn't get out of. I had to wait for it to blow over.

I was in and out of terrible sleep for a few hours before I finally got up. And I knew what to do. I kind of felt terrible about it, but I had to go back down to the ocean. I had to see Blue again for myself.

I took my phone and stuffed it into my pocket, but I saw a notification first. Marc had texted again, asking if I was okay. I'd have to answer that later. I got dressed and I snuck toward the front of the house. I heard Nadia yelling that it was her turn to use the remote control, and Masha saying she just needed to sit for ten minutes. She was probably cleaning up a mess, or changing Hannah, or taking a break, playing games on her phone.

As I stepped out the front door, Caleb was sitting on the doorstep again. I guess it was going to be harder to get out than I wanted. I started back into the house. I'd have to sneak out the back.

"What are you doing here?" he asked, his fingers playing with his shoelaces.

I wanted to keep moving, not saying a thing. But I couldn't quite do it. My haze had lifted enough. "I could ask you the same thing. Shouldn't you be in school by now?"

He looked forward. "I have to go to the therapist this morning."

I paused. I didn't know that Caleb saw a therapist. Why would he do that? Did anyone mention that before and I just missed it?

"Okay," I said. "I had a rough night, so my dad let me stay home today."

"Cool," he said, a smile crossing his face. "Want to do something?"

"Not right now," I said. He was a decent kid, and quiet enough when he was by himself. But I wasn't going to stick around. "I've got to go."

"To school?" he asked. Why did he have to keep talking? "'Cause you're really late."

"Yeah," I lied, because that wasn't a bad cover story. "I'd better hurry up."

"Where's your backpack?" he asked.

Curse that kid. He was observant.

"I don't need it today," I said. But then realized that if I told my dad I went to school, then I could go to the beach first for however long I needed. As long as I eventually made it to school, I'd be fine. And I should probably get to school. Mom would want me to. "Never mind," I said. "I do need it. Thanks." And I stepped back inside. After sneaking up to my room to grab it, I texted my dad that I had woken up and was going to school. Then I slid out the door.

My dad texted back.

> Okay. I can give you a ride if you want.

I didn't answer. And I still hadn't answered Marc.

I sped down the hill and saw Blue in the distance.

Part of me was sad that the experts weren't there. They had probably been there all of yesterday. But today, it was like Blue wasn't important enough for them. Not worth getting up for. Or maybe they just wanted their coffee first. But it still made me sad. Maybe they thought coffee was more important than Blue.

I jumped off my bike and went down to him.

He was surrounded with caution tape—an area a lot bigger than necessary. They really didn't want anyone getting close. I guess they were serious about the danger a beached whale could cause.

I pulled out my phone and took some pictures; it was the scientist in me. I always document what I see of ocean life. But mostly I just wanted to remember Blue.

I hated seeing him there, completely still. If only I had arrived earlier. Or maybe if we had tried the boats idea or gotten everyone on the island to help push. I know those ideas were kind of stupid, but anything would be better than this. I clearly hadn't helped enough. I just wasn't sure what I was supposed to have done differently.

Sometimes I wondered that about my mom. Could I have done anything for her? Could I have noticed problems with her heart earlier? Maybe if I was a better scientist I would have noticed and insisted she visit the doctor. Or maybe if I was a better daughter, she never would have left my dad in the first place and then we definitely would have noticed.

Those thoughts might not even be true, but I thought them.

I took more pics of the whale. I got both faraway shots and close-up shots. I got good pictures of his closed eyes, his baleen, his blowhole, those fins. I knew I was going overboard, but I just did it.

And then I sat down on the beach. Just me and a big dead whale.

"I'm sorry," I said.

I have to admit, I wished Blue would speak back. That he would say that there was nothing more I could have done. That he would tell me about where he was now and if my mom was there. That he would explain how he died, why he died, why I shouldn't be so sad for him. But he didn't. He wasn't there.

It felt like a time I should cry, but I just didn't have the tears. It wasn't the first time my tears were all dried up. "I really did try."

"Willa?" a voice came from the ocean.

Meg. Part of me was thrilled, but the other part didn't want to answer. I had let her down. She had asked me to help Blue.

I took in a deep breath. "Hey, Meg," I said and then the words tumbled out. "I'm so sorry, but he didn't make it. I tried. I really did. I called in all the experts. I kept his skin wet. I called in my friends. I did everything I could."

"Oh, little human," Meg said and then fell quiet.

I wondered if she was silent because she was mourning or because she was disappointed in me.

I wouldn't blame her. I was disappointed in me.

Then I heard another long moan. Then another. I wanted to call like that too.

Finally, Meg spoke. "I knew him. He was a beautiful whale, big and gentle. Just a little younger than me. His pod is heartbroken. They said that he was struck by a boat."

A boat. I hated that.

In order to kill a whale as big as Blue, it was probably a monstrous ship. Like a cruise ship or a shipping vessel. Yesterday, I read an article that said more than eighty whales are hit every year just along the coast of California, Oregon, and Washington. When you understand the small numbers we have of some of these whales, that's a lot.

What a way to go for a creature with no known natural predators. Dying of accidents caused by people.

I sat on the rocks and looked at Blue.

"How many are in his pod?"

"Three others, two females and a calf."

Somewhere out there is a calf without a father. Even though I had already thought that might happen, hearing that it was true made my shoulders slump and my head drop. I wanted to melt into the beach below my feet.

"I wish I could carry your sadness a little while," I said. "But my own is too heavy right now. I can't carry much more."

Another long call.

I gave one too. It was long and ugly and I hope it wasn't insulting, but it felt good.

Then silence.

"I'm sorry, Willa," Meg eventually said. "This hurts. It hurts you. It hurts me. I have lived long enough now to know that the sadness is normal, that the darkness will lift, that though we will always miss our loved ones, at some point we will feel like we have been lifted from the blackness at the bottom of the sea towards the sunlight." She paused to let out another call. "But right now, it just hurts."

Another call.

I gave one too.

"But it isn't your fault, Willa," Meg said. "You did what you could. Nobody blames you. Don't blame yourself. That is a pain you don't have to feel. A pain that doesn't take you anywhere."

I nodded. I understood what she was saying, but it was hard to believe.

"Hey," I heard someone say behind me. I recognized the voice.

And it wasn't Marc.

CHAPTER 26

Follower

Willa Twitchell, Journal #5, today

Fish have instincts. Even when they're young, small fish seem to know when a predator is around. And on the other side, predators have instincts too. Like sharks have extra senses that help them feel vibrations through the water that help them find their food.

Humans don't have as many instincts. We have to learn. One way is by watching and following others.

~~~~~~~~~~~~~~~~~~

"What is that?" Caleb stood right behind me, pointing at Blue, his mouth wide open. "It's huge."

I looked at him, then back at Blue. "What are you doing here?"

Caleb faltered a little, entranced by the huge whale. "Back on the doorstep, you were saying stuff kind of funny and I was worried about . . . I just wanted to see if you were . . ." Again he trailed off. "So I got on my bike and tried to catch up with you."

I found it really interesting that he was worried about me. It made me feel bad. The kid probably had enough to worry about without adding a stepsister to the mix.

Caleb looked me square in the eye again. "This isn't school. And what *is* that?" he repeated, still staring at Blue.

He shouldn't be here, but I could tell I wasn't going to get anywhere with him until I answered the question about Blue. I couldn't blame him. If I were him, I'd want to know too. "It's one of the largest creatures in the world and it died last night."

Caleb's shoulders fell. "That's so sad," he said. "How did it get here?"

"I don't want to explain right now," I said.

"You said you were going to school, but this isn't school," Caleb repeated.

"Sorry, Caleb," I said, putting my arm around his shoulder. "I really am going to school. I just stopped by the beach first."

"Why?" he asked. "Who were you talking to? Do you have a phone with those invisible talking things?" He poked my ear to check for a bluetooth.

"No." I looked out to the water. "I was—" I stopped. What was I going to say? All the excuses I thought up would sound even more ridiculous than the truth. So I told him. He was a seven-year-old boy and, according to what he'd said, he had seen me down here talking before. What could it hurt? "I was talking to a whale named Meg. I come down here and tell her all of the things that go wrong in my life and she helps me. She tells me stories and stuff. But today, we were both just really sad because of the dead whale." I looked over at Blue, huge, magnificent, and lifeless.

"And what were those weird noises you made?" he asked. He must have heard my sorrow call when I was trying to match Meg. "Was that Japanese?"

I shook my head. Definitely not Japanese. "No," I said.

"I didn't think so," he said with a nervous laugh.

"Meg and I were just sad."

He surveyed the waves. "Where is the whale you talk to?" he asked, looking around.

"I'm not exactly sure," I admitted. "But she's out there." I pointed at the water. "She can hear me from miles away."

One of Caleb's brows dipped. He was having trouble with this idea. "Miles?"

I just nodded.

"You talk to a whale that tells you stories that is miles away."

"Yes," I admitted. "Named Meg."

"And you speak whale language?" he asked. Maybe I shouldn't have told him about Meg. Maybe some lie would have been better. He had a ton of questions.

"No," I said, "we just speak English."

He studied my face for a few seconds, then smiled. "I wish I talked to whales." I wasn't expecting that. Not at all. "One time I had an invisible friend. He was a dog named Potato Chip and he had a unicorn horn."

It took me so off guard, I actually laughed. That was strange and good after all the sadness. I wasn't sure if he thought that

Meg was pretend or not, but I did like the idea of a uni-dog named Potato Chip.

Caleb moved right up next to me. "Can you teach me to talk to whales?"

And I think he meant it. Again, I wasn't expecting that.

"Please," he said.

Yep. He meant it.

And he believed me. Not only that, but he wanted to talk to whales too. It made me feel good that the first person I really told about Meg didn't make fun of me or call me crazy. He wished he had a Meg of his own. "I don't think that I can. I'm not entirely sure how it works." That was true, but it kind of made me sad. It sounded like Caleb could really use a whale.

"Willa! Caleb!" Our names sounded like a whisper through all the wind, but that was just because they were coming from far away. I looked around. Masha was yelling from up the slope. "Get up here—now!"

Busted.

CHAPTER 27

Friends, but No Matching Necklaces

Willa Twitchell, Journal #5, today

It doesn't matter what species you are, almost all mamas get upset when they can't find their kids.

~~~~~~~~~~

"What were you thinking?" Masha asked as she drove. She had thrown both of our bikes in the back of the minivan, which wasn't easy to do. I think that put her in an even worse mood. "Caleb, you cannot ride to the ocean without someone with you, let alone go down that dangerous trail."

The minivan smelled like old ketchup and Nadia's stinky sandals. I wanted to roll down my window, but I wasn't sure I was brave enough to ask permission. I just turned the car vent towards me.

"Willa was there," he said, like that explained everything.

"Willa is in trouble too," Masha said, stopping at a light

and letting out a huff. "Now we're going to be late to your appointment because we have to drop Willa at school first."

That's right. Caleb had some sort of therapy appointment. I wanted to ask about it, but I was pretty sure now was not the time.

"I can just ride my bike," I said quietly. I felt like a minnow making a suggestion to a hungry tiger shark.

"But if I let you do that," Masha said, "will you end up at school or the beach?" By the tone she used she didn't expect me to answer that question.

"Did you know that Willa can talk to whales?" Caleb asked, enthusiastically changing the subject. It was like he couldn't tell how mad his mom was. Or maybe he didn't care. He just launched into something he was excited about.

Masha glanced at me but didn't answer Caleb.

"I want to talk to whales," Nadia said, bouncing in her booster seat. "I can't talk to any animals yet." Like that was a superpower she would get when she got older.

Garth raised both hands, his three-year-old legs dangling from his car seat. "I talk whale," Garth said with a huge smile on his face. Then he growled. Did he think whales growled? Cute. He said something else, but I don't think any of us understood him.

Hannah laughed from her seat like she was in on the conversation.

"Willa says she can't teach me," Caleb explained. "I already asked. But she goes to the beach and talks to a whale named, um, . . . something I forgot."

"Meg," I corrected, before I could stop myself.

Masha looked away from the windshield at me again, then back.

Caleb kept talking. "And the whale can tell her stories. And she tells the whale a lot of stuff." Caleb moved his arms with his words and his gestures were getting more animated. "And they are best friends and they have best friend necklaces."

What? That got weird fast. "We don't have necklaces." Again, I chimed in. What was I doing? I was practically admitting that I talked to whales.

Caleb pointed at me. "You should. I saw friend necklaces at the store and best friends wear them. She is your best friend, right?"

I wiggled my head in a noncommittal way. I guess I hadn't really thought about it before.

"I want a whale necklace," Nadia said, holding out her hand like I had some in my pocket that I was about to give out.

"Whale," Garth added and bounced up and down in his car seat.

"Willa," Masha said, "do you really talk to whales?" She was looking at me again, and I think she was trying hard to keep her tone normal.

I didn't know how to answer. Would she think I was crazy? Or was she really curious? Would she believe like Caleb? Probably not. But what if she did? I couldn't tell. I haven't studied humans like I have marine creatures.

So I settled on, "Kind of."

I held my breath, waiting for her to get me in trouble, to

get upset for telling her children what she thought were lies. For being crazy.

"A lot or just once?" Masha asked.

Well, she wasn't upset yet.

Again, I didn't know how to answer. "I guess a lot."

"Are the whales nice or mean?" I really didn't expect this many questions. Or questions like this. Where was this going?

"There's just one whale and she's really nice."

Masha nodded. Apparently, that was a good answer. She didn't say anything else about the whale but the kids in the back seat didn't stop talking about them for the rest of the ride. "I want to keep a whale for a pet," Nadia said.

"They're too big," Caleb said. "It's not like you can just keep it in the bathtub."

"I'll have a small whale," Nadia clarified.

"Whale. Whale. Whale," Garth agreed.

"I saw a whale at our house," Nadia said.

"No, you didn't," Caleb said.

"Yes, I did. It was hiding in the shed," Nadia said.

"That doesn't even make sense," Caleb said, but was laughing while he said it. And the conversation kept going until Hannah blew spit out her mouth and laughed. Then everyone giggled together.

"Have a good day at school," Masha said as I got out. She says stuff like that sometimes, but she's often too busy to even look at me when she says it. But this time Masha looked at me. I think she was still trying to find out more about me. Like maybe she wasn't sure what she thought about a girl who talks to a whale.

CHAPTER 28

Like We Used To

Willa Twitchell, Journal #5, today

The wind is blowing furiously today, throwing ocean spray everywhere, and even making it hard to walk straight. That happens sometimes.

But it smells so fresh. I love it. So I'm sitting snuggled behind the protection of the cliff. I've read that the ocean—well, especially the plants in the ocean—make over 80% of the world's oxygen. That means that all of us are breathing ocean air right now. Whether you are close to the ocean or not.

I'm feeling really grateful because today, I really needed to breathe some fresh air.

#ThankYouPlankton #IReallyNeededThis

I slipped in while Mr. Norton was discussing some dude

who was a general in the War of 1812. I was going to have to look at someone's notes because I missed more than just his name. I could tell that Mr. Norton was annoyed with having to stop his lecture to take my tardy slip from the office so I tried to do it as fast and quiet as possible.

I succeeded at fast. Not at quiet.

After handing him the note, I turned so quickly that I ran smack into his podium, then tumbled to the floor. As if I didn't have enough to worry about.

Feeling stupid, I looked up into the shocked face of Lizzy Wallace.

"Are you okay?" she asked. I didn't answer but popped up and bolted to my seat while the kids around snickered.

My ears were hot and my pulse was racing as I sat down and tried to look like I didn't care about what had just happened. I pulled out my notebook to take notes, but couldn't pay attention to anything.

I glanced over at Marc and he gave a tight-lipped kind of smile. I had no idea what that meant. Was that a good thing or a bad thing? There was so little expression in it. Was he embarrassed to be friends with such a klutz? Or maybe we weren't really friends again. Or maybe he felt sorry for me because of my full-on freak-out at the beach. I had been a wreck. I couldn't even respond to people. He must have thought I had lost it. Or maybe he was still mad at me because of the way I just barged into his home and asked personal questions. It's not like he ever said he forgave me for that. All I had to indicate that we might still be friends is that he came to help me with Blue. And that hadn't turned out well.

The bell rang eventually. Everyone started gathering their things and talking. I couldn't get myself to look at Marc again. Slowly, I put my notebook back in my backpack. I took a deep breath. I just needed to make it to the next class. It wasn't too far away. I could make it there and then I could skip lunch and hide in the library, then only two more classes.

I could do this.

"Hey," Marc said, standing in front of me, "let's go." He had the same tight-lipped smile.

I didn't know what to say or think. So I stood up and followed him out of the classroom.

"Sorry about yesterday," he said as we walked down the hall. "I mean, about the whale." It all came out awkward, but he was trying.

"I'm sorry, too."

"I can't focus," he said. "I'm not even sure what Mr. Norton was talking about today."

"Me neither," I admitted.

"I've been worried like crazy about you," he said.

We headed further down the hallway. "Worried about me?"

"Yeah," he said. "Want to grab a cookie for lunch, like we used to get after school when we were in elementary?" Memories rushed back to me. Before I moved, sometimes we went to Eric's Grocery and bought two cookies from the bakery. They had the best ones. The kind where there was at least as much frosting as cookie. I think a little bit of happiness was included with each cookie. "I'll pay," he said.

It wouldn't be much of a lunch. But it would be frosting and sprinkles and a friend. "Okay," I said.

CHAPTER 29

Cookies

Willa Twitchell, Journal #5, today

Swedish Fish are red and about one to two inches long. They don't swim but they do float, and they taste good with movie theater popcorn. They aren't actually made in Sweden. They're made in Canada. Weird, I know. But I still love them.

The only thing that's better are frosted sugar cookies.

And a friend.

This journal entry was brought to you by an empty stomach.

#SeriouslySoHungry

~~~~~~~~~~~~~~~~~~~~~~~~~~~~~~

"I figured something out last night," Marc said as we walked away from the school toward the store. It was only a block and a half away. I had barely made it through gym. And Marc made it through Spanish. We met by the side doors. "And it's been eating at me. Then when you didn't show up at school again, I was scared."

"Scared for what?" I asked, matching Marc's stride. I didn't think we'd be talking about Marc's fears.

He tightened the straps on his backpack. "I think I finally understand something I didn't get before." He looked at me and squished his mouth to one side.

"I'm so confused," I admitted.

He just stared out at the road, then at me. "I was so mad at you for prying into my life, for asking about stuff I didn't want to tell you the answers to," he said. "I freaked out. I have reasons for that, but that's not my point." He kicked a rock, sending it bouncing across the sidewalk then over the curb.

I kept walking.

"It's just that I saw you melt down yesterday," Marc said. "When you found out that the whale was dead, you collapsed. I mean, I knew you loved sea animals, but that seemed like a lot. I may have even thought you were overreacting." He kicked another rock. We could see the parking lot to Eric's Grocery. "But then I mentioned it to my mom, and she said that she thought you had your reasons. She said that everyone always has their reasons."

I wasn't sure where he was going with this.

"And I've been thinking about it all last night and this morning. Which was nice to have something interesting to think about in English for a change." He half laughed at himself. "Why would you be so upset when a whale died? Why would it bother you so bad? And then I got it. At least I think I did."

We reached the parking lot and a woman got out of her car not too far from us. "I'll tell you the rest in a minute," he said, nodding just a little at the woman. I was grateful for that. I didn't know if I wanted to talk about this in front of other people.

We came to the store and went inside. It isn't like one of those giant grocery stores I've seen on the mainland, but it's pretty good-sized. We walked to the bakery and I picked a big sugar cookie with blue frosting and rainbow sprinkles, just like I used to. Marc went for the chocolate chip cookie. I felt a moment of guilt letting him pay for them, but it was only a dollar and he insisted. Plus, I hadn't brought any money.

Instead of sitting on two of the only eight chairs inside the grocery store, we went walking down the road. Just like old times. We'd probably end up at the ocean just in time to walk back to school. But this way we didn't have to worry about people over-hearing us.

"I think what happened to the whale bothered you so much, . . ." Marc continued. He hadn't even taken a bite of his cookie yet. I, on the other hand, probably already had blue frosting-stained teeth. And it tasted so good. ". . . because you just really have a hard time dealing with," he almost whispered, "death. Because of your mom."

I stopped chewing.

And I was so glad we weren't sitting in those chairs at the grocery, or at school, or next to that lady who was getting out of her car.

I went back to my cookie. Frosting and cookies are powerful, but not enough to stop sniffles. But they at least held back the full-on bawl.

Marc just awkwardly looked at me for a moment. There I was, all sniffly and taking bites of my cookie, hoping that it would somehow help.

"I'm sorry I didn't get it," he said, and ran his fingers nervously though his floppy hair. "I knew it would be hard, and I knew it happened. I mean, people find out about this stuff. There was a reason you came back. But somehow I thought you got over it." He stopped and choked up a little. He folded his arms across his chest. "But then I thought about what's bothering me, and that's not going away. And I thought if I lost my mom, I don't think I'd ever stop being sad."

I didn't say anything. And I let a few tears out. Maybe the cookie was losing its power. I was already halfway through.

He did get it. At least part of it.

"And I don't know what to say other than it just has to feel terrible. And I'm sorry." He looked like he might try to hug me or something, but he didn't. He probably had no better idea of what to do in these situations than I did.

So we just walked. And I tried not to cry. "You're right," I said. "It feels worse than anything."

He nodded and we turned down Mill Street. It would end at Mill Park Beach. Marc finally started into his cookie.

"But you never talk about it," he said, his mouth kind of full.

"Who wants to talk about stuff like that?" I threw my hands up. "It's not like someone says, 'Good morning' and I'm going to respond that it isn't good because I can't stop thinking about my dead mom. People don't want to hear that."

"But it is okay to talk about it," Marc said, and took another bite.

"But . . ." I started.

"But what?" he asked.

"It's hard to do," I said. "Like you. You still haven't told me what's bothering you. Why you can't be on the swim team. Why you won't let me pay for it. Why something about Sofia bothers you."

He shook his head. "I know." We walked further. He kicked another rock then took another bite. My cookie was long gone. "It's just . . . that's my business."

"See," I said, "it's not that easy to do."

Marc nodded. "I'm sorry," he said. "I'm just going through something and I can't figure out how to fix it. You're the only one who's even asking about it, but I just can't talk about it yet." He shuffled. "Nash doesn't ask. Luke doesn't." He pounded one fist into his open hand, but only a few times before stopping. "But you do. And you ask all the right questions. And I think you might figure it out and then . . ." He stopped. We weren't walking anymore.

I waited. "Then what?" I finally asked.

"Then you might not be my friend anymore."

"Not be your friend?" I asked. "Why would I not be your friend?"

He just shook his head.

"Listen," I said, "I'm your friend—no matter what your

problem is. And I need you to be my friend." I was surprised I was being this honest. "And I understand not wanting to talk about stuff, but when you're ready, I'll listen." I sounded like my dad. "I may even understand a little." I pushed him playfully on the shoulder, just like we used to do a long time ago.

"Thanks," Marc said and pushed me back. It was probably a little strong, but I didn't mind. "But is there like . . . anything else I can do?" he asked.

I took a few more steps. "You already bought me one of the best cookies on the island," I said, and flashed him my blue teeth.

He smiled. And then I told him all about my mom.

CHAPTER 30

What to Do with a Dead Whale?

Willa Twitchell, Journal #4, one year ago

I've heard all sorts of rumors and crazy ideas about the ocean. Like it's deepest in the middle, or it's blue because it reflects the sky. Both false. But when I hear a rumor, I have to look it up to see if it's true or not.

~~~~~~~~~~~~~~~~~~~

By my last class, everyone was talking about a huge dead whale that had washed up. I think it probably started yesterday, but the news spread like algae bloom.

And there was a rumor about Blue. A rumor I hated. A rumor I had to know if it was true.

When the last bell rang, I jumped on my bike and rode like a sailfish.

Marc was right behind me.

But as we pulled up to the turnout off the highway, something was very different. Cars. Lots of them. There were never cars here.

We leapt down the rocks, looking at the site of our normally empty beach overrun with spectators and gawkers.

Coming down, I almost bumped right into an older lady who had stopped to catch her breath on the way back up. That was awkward.

I figured that people would eventually find out about it but it still felt nuts. Nobody was here this morning and now BOOM! Word travels fast on an island.

I didn't like it.

Blue wasn't a spectacle. He was an amazing creature who had passed away from a sad accident.

The crowd was taking pictures and pointing. To them it was like they were on a whale watch again. But it shouldn't be. It shouldn't be anything close.

He looked worse than he did before, all limp and lying still in the hot sun.

Inside the caution tape, a group of people took pictures and measurements and held clipboards and talked. They didn't look very experty, no special uniforms or anything. And the one guy's long hair, jacket, and boots made him look a lot more ready to break out into a guitar solo than worry about beached whales.

"Your whale doesn't smell so good," Marc said, his nose wrinkling. He was right. Now that the sun had been shining on him for hours, and he had been dead for a day and a half, he had started to stink a little. And it would only get worse.

"You wouldn't either if it were you," I said. Then I sniffed. "Maybe you don't smell so good now."

He playfully punched me in the shoulder. I was proud of myself that I could joke about it, even a little. Yesterday morning I had been a wreck. "Maybe it's *you* and not the whale," I teased.

Another punch, this time a little less playful.

I walked right up to the caution tape. "Excuse me," I said to the closest woman, "can I talk to you for a minute?" No one inside the tape seemed too bothered by the smell. Maybe they were used to it.

A tan woman with black curly hair turned around. "Umm, I guess." She motioned to the man she was working with to wait for her. "What's up?" There was a clip to her voice that made it clear she was busy.

"Hi, I'm Willa Twitchell." I put out my hand. "I found this whale and called it in."

She put both of her hands up to indicate they weren't clean enough for a shake. "Okay." And that's all she said. No "thank you." Nothing. She seemed snooty. I didn't like her.

"I heard a rumor I need to confirm," I said. "Or hopefully not." The idea of the rumor bothered me and I needed to find out how true it was.

"I'm sorry," she said, "I don't have time to—"

She was going to cut me off like I was a little kid asking stupid questions. "My mother was a marine biologist—" I blurted out. "—Maylan Twitchell." The stings started up but then Marc put his hand on my shoulder and calmness poured over the pain.

The woman was silent for a moment. "I knew your mom. She

taught me at Northwest. I'm sorry." Probably anyone who worked with sea creatures in this area knew my mom.

"I'm sorry too," I said, but now she was listening. "What's going to happen next? To the whale?" Something was going to have to be done about a huge dead whale on the beach. And I didn't like what I had heard.

"Well," the woman said, "it's complicated. This beach is hard to get to, and far away from town. It doesn't leave us many choices of what to do with the whale. I think the best thing to do is just to let it decompose on the beach, but some of the residents and the city don't like that idea. So, we are going to let the city propose how to dispose of the whale."

Decompose? *Dispose?* I hated the idea of both words. But the second one especially. Like Blue was a broken piece of furniture or a gum wrapper or something. But neither of these ideas were the rumor.

"Could we bury it?" I asked. That seemed like the best option to me.

"Well, this is tricky," she said. "Sometimes we can bury the animals, but this cove doesn't have access for a backhoe to get down here. Even then, I'm not sure this beach is big enough to bury this whale and not have it come back up again as the beach erodes."

I had thought of that. "What about burying it somewhere else?" I asked.

"We'd need huge boats or a giant truck and some cranes to get it off the beach." I tried to picture what they would look like, giant metal cranes over my cove. "And access that way would be hard too. We don't have many options."

Marc piped in, "I heard they were thinking about cutting it up and towing the pieces out to sea, or even exploding it." There were the rumors. Nasty, gross rumors.

"Maybe," she said, "but I hope it's not the explosion. We don't want Oregon in 1976 all over again."

"No," I said, though I didn't know about Oregon in 1976. I just didn't want exploding.

She smiled. "Well, that is what the city meeting is for. They are going to hold it next week. I guess that's the regular time the council meets and this whale isn't going anywhere." She pointed at Blue. "Go and tell them what's on your mind." She only confirmed what we'd heard.

I had to go to that meeting. There had to be a better way. Blue needed to have a respectable send-off. He was special to someone out there in the ocean. Missed. He was special to me. He needed to be treated right, remembered right.

"I'd bet we're going to be at the city meeting," Marc said.

I nodded. "But what are we going to tell them?"

I had no idea, but Blue wasn't going to be exploded. Not on my watch.

CHAPTER 31

Whalesplosion

Willa Twitchell, Journal #5, today

Today I heard a story that I really, really, really, really, really, really, really, hoped wasn't true.
It was.

Marc and I came in through my front door and walked past Nadia and Garth watching cartoons. An empty popcorn bowl lay on the couch between them.

I didn't even slow down. We had something to look up. I needed to understand all of our options. Even the bad ones.

I moved into the study where the family computer sat on a white desk. I was a girl on a mission.

"Okay," I said, sitting at the desk. I typed in *Oregon whale 1976* and it worked. There was clip after clip of the same news broadcast. "Which one do we choose?" I asked.

No one answered.

I turned around. Where was Marc? He was walking right behind me a few seconds ago.

I peeked back into the TV room and Marc was talking to Nadia and Garth. Garth leaned over the armrest. Nadia held the popcorn bowl and stood on the couch so she could talk to Marc face to face. Caleb was there too. I hadn't noticed him at first because he was playing with baby Hannah in the corner.

"Come on, Marc," I said. "What's the hold up?"

He raised his hand. "Be right there." He turned to Nadia. "So we went to investigate and there were professionals there and they said that they are trying to figure out what to do with the whale. And one option is to explode it."

"No way," Caleb said, his eyes big. "Like a whalesplosion?"

Nadia was pulling popcorn kernels out of the bowl and trying to throw them in Marc's mouth while he spoke. Nobody was watching television anymore.

Marc closed his mouth quickly, swallowing a laugh. "Whalesplosion? Maybe," he said, leaning down towards Garth to avoid Nadia's kernels. He was really great to deal with all their kookiness. "That's why we're here. We're going to look into it."

"Whalesplosion," Nadia said and made an explosion sound. Soon all of my stepsiblings were doing it.

"Come on, Marc," I said, pulling on his arm.

"Okay, I've got to go," he told my stepsibs and let me drag him toward the study.

"Bye," they all said, waving the best they could without stopping their explosions.

When I finally succeeded in bringing Marc into the next room, I closed the door behind us. No use trying to research with utter chaos popping their heads in.

"Sorry," Marc said, "your brother asked you a question and I don't think you heard it."

"Really?" He had asked something? Then again, when I got super focused on something I sometimes didn't even notice that I needed to eat. The idea of an exploding whale had me super, super focused.

Soon enough we were both sitting in front of the computer looking at the search results.

"Whoa," Marc said. "Someone actually exploded a whale. Click on it."

I clicked. The video looked old. Like when-my-Grandpa-Twitchell-wore-bell-bottoms old. Some reporter with thick blond hair started, "It had to be said that the Oregon State Highway Division had a whale of a problem on its hands. It had a stinking whale of a problem." Very punny. I rolled my eyes, but Marc laughed.

The reported continued, "What to do with one forty-five-foot, eight-ton whale, dead on arrival on a beach near Florence?" In the background was a heap of a whale. Much smaller than Blue, but still big. The poor thing. I wondered how it died, and whether the news ever wanted to do a story on it when it was alive and amazing.

"It had been so long since a whale had washed up in Lane County that no one remembered how to get rid of one. In selecting its battle plan, the highway division decided that it couldn't be buried, for it would soon be uncovered. It couldn't be cut up and then buried because no one wanted to cut it up, and it couldn't be burned."

Burned. I hadn't thought of that. Would that be a proper goodbye? Maybe. But how long would a whale with that much blubber burn for? Could you even light it on fire?

"So dynamite it was," the reporter said. And then the video showed the dynamite. Case after case of it.

I shuddered.

"Tell me this is fake." I said.

"I don't think it is," Marc said, shaking his head.

The reporter explained how they were going to do it. The plan was to completely annihilate the dead whale. Most pieces would simply be totally disintegrated, and what was left they hoped that the seagulls, crabs, and other scavengers would pick up off the beach.

"Whoa," Marc said. "Okay, that is a pretty crazy way to go."

I shook my head. "It's wrong."

According to the newscast, some seventy-five people came to watch the whale explode.

"I would totally go watch that," Marc said.

"Gross," I said and hit him on the arm.

"Oh, you'd be there too," he said. I tried to hit him on the arm again, but he moved.

The reporter talked more. I still couldn't believe they were actually going to do it. The camera pulled back for the long shot. The sand, the water, the whale, the dune of grass waving in the wind. It all looked peaceful. And then—

BOOM!

They did it.

For real.

Sand rocketed in every direction, filling the screen in a split second. An explosion. A legitimate whale explosion on a beach.

"Whoa," Marc said again.

And then . . . it sounded like it was raining. The people around the camera started talking, and then their voices rose to shouts. The raining got harder.

I gasped.

Blubber.

It was raining blubber.

Pieces of the whale were falling from the sky.

"Oh, no," I said.

"It's raining . . . whale," Marc said in disbelief.

The camera cut back to the reporter. "Our camera stopped rolling after the blast. The humor of the situation suddenly gave way to a run for survival as huge chunks of whale blubber fell everywhere."

"This is insane," Marc said.

One huge piece totally destroyed the top of a car.

"We've got to do better than this," I said. I would not let anyone explode Blue.

CHAPTER 32

A Package

Willa Twitchell, Journal #5, today

I got something today that I didn't expect. Something I'm not sure I'm ready for.

~~~~~~~~~~~~~~~~~~~~~~~~~~~~~~~~~~~~~~

A package.

I just stared at it, a white box with papers taped to the top. It was from Japan and addressed to me. From Kanagawa, where I used to live.

It was like a gift from the past.

Masha had brought it in to the office and was watching over my shoulder. My dad was there, too. In fact, I think Masha got it earlier and had waited for my dad. Marc had to go home and I was still trying to think of what to do about Blue.

"Is it your birthday day?" Nadia asked, spinning on the office chair.

I cut the tape and looked inside, so curious that I didn't answer Nadia's question. On top was an envelope with my name on it. I recognized the handwriting right away. Chihiro, the woman who'd cared for me when I couldn't be with my mom.

I lifted up the letter and found a few boxes of chocolate Pocky sticks, and a small bag of Konpeitōs, my favorite sugar candy.

"Can I have some of these?" Nadia asked.

"I want some too," Caleb said. Then Garth entered the mix. They'd all come into the office.

I didn't want to share. These were for me, pieces from a great time in my life. But I wasn't sure how I was going to have kids see candy and not try some. I handed a box of Pocky sticks to Masha. "You guys can share these." All the kids jumped up and down with excitement.

"You can have one now," Masha said, "but the rest we save until after dinner. Tell your sister thank you."

They all said thank you in near unison. It almost made giving up some Japanese treats worth it.

But when I pulled out the rest of the candy, there was something underneath, wrapped in paper. A book. I pulled it out and unwrapped it. And I almost stopped breathing.

A simple, leather-bound book. I touched it softly, like it was an antique. If it was what I thought, to me it was priceless.

"You got a book for your birthday day?" Nadia asked.

I think I nodded, but I'm not completely sure. I opened the first page and saw my mom's handwriting. It was like she was here.

It's time to start another journal, but this one is going to be different than all those before. In this one, my life has changed forever. I have a little girl.

I shut it. My emotions were so jumbled and so big that I knew if I read more I would probably melt. I just held it for a minute then set it down. I would read it later. When I was ready. And I would read it over and over, just like her others.

I opened the letter from Chihiro:

Dear Willa,

This journal was found in a small drawer in your mother's office. You should have it.

I have been thinking about you recently as we have been planning here for Obon. You went to a few Obon festivals here with your mother. Do you remember? It's the holiday where we honor our ancestors. We dance for them, we feed them, we spend time thanking them? This one is extra special for me because I have been missing your mother a lot.

Your mother will be close in my heart the whole time.

I have included a lantern for you. We light the lanterns so that our ancestors can find us. If you'd like, you can light the lantern and then express gratitude for your mother. And she can find you.

Know that I will be dancing my very best for her here in Japan.

I miss you very much. I hope you are healthy and happy in America.

Best wishes,
Chihiro

I remembered Obon. There were lanterns set up around a

podium and musicians and dancers. So many dancers. I remembered yakatori chicken and chocolate-dipped bananas. Even though it was a festival for the dead, I don't think I saw one person crying there. They were happy. All of my memories of Obon were happy.

I checked the bottom of the box and sure enough, there was a paper lantern all folded up.

I loved Chihiro.

I sat there looking through my gifts and wondering if I should read the journal.

Soon, it was only my dad and I left in the room. Now that there weren't any more presents to open and the kids had candy, they had run off. Masha went with them.

"That's an amazing gift," Dad said.

I nodded.

He sat down in the chair Nadia had been spinning in before. "Sorry to leave you this morning. You were just sleeping so sound I figured you might need a little bit of a break. Are you doing okay?"

I put the lantern back in the box. "Yeah, actually. Much better." I think my talk with Marc had really made a difference. Or the cookie. Or both.

He scooted a little closer. "I have something else I want to talk about. You took that whale dying really hard," he said.

I nodded.

"And it's been tough to move back here and to have lost your mom."

I nodded again. I didn't like where this was going.

"And Masha said," he paused for a moment, "that you talk to whales."

Oh no. I'm not sure how I didn't see that coming, but I didn't. And I wasn't ready to talk to him about Meg.

I shrugged.

"Look," he said, "that may be a good thing to do. I don't know." He rubbed his face. "I mean, I know you've been through something really hard, but I don't know what's the best way to deal with it. I'm not a professional counselor or anything."

I looked at him, wondering what he was trying to say. I kind of wished he would just go back to doing cheesy magic tricks.

"Which actually is what I wanted to talk to you about," he said and took a deep breath. "Willa, when I saw you the other day, on that beach, unable to move, I knew that your pain was intense." He scratched his big brown beard. "Some pain in life is expected. Kind of like sometimes you'll get a bruise or you'll scrape your knee. You don't run to the emergency room for those things. But some pain needs help from a specialist. If you needed stitches or your appendix burst, you'd need to see a doctor who could help you." He paused again. "What I'm trying to say is that maybe it's time that you saw a therapist."

He tried to explain why this was a good idea but all I kept hearing was that my dad thought I was broken.

CHAPTER 33

An Idea

**Maylan Twitchell, Journal #13,
twelve years ago**

Willa took her first steps today. I had to pick her up so many times. She just kept falling. It was so discouraging to her, but for me I knew it would turn out well. She just always has to keep trying. And know that I'll always be there to help. And her dad. And lots of others.

~~~~~~~~~~~~~~~~~~~~~~~~

"How is the blue whale pod doing?" I asked across the ocean. There were a few people milling about Blue, so I stayed by the tide pools. I didn't worry about the people hearing me talk. They were far enough away and the wind was whipping so loudly around us I'm sure they couldn't hear a thing. And unless I was wrong, no one else seemed to be able to hear Meg.

I think Meg rolled a little before answering. "Hurting," she said. "They started a mourning song and the pod has been singing it ever since. They trade off who sings, but there is always someone singing. And they won't leave until they are finished."

"How long will that last?" I asked. Even though it was amazingly sad, I kind of liked the idea. They sang their sadness. I, unfortunately, was a terrible singer. But the idea of a tribute like that sounded nice.

"I don't know," Meg said. "Maybe a couple of days."

Those poor whales.

"And how are you doing, Willa?" Meg asked.

"I'm okay," I said, walking out on the edge of the pools. "I still hurt too, but it really helps that I think Marc and I are definitely friends again. We had a great talk, and a cookie. Both were really good."

"What's a cookie?" Meg asked.

The fact that she had to ask that question made me wonder if Meg had ever really known happiness. I tried to think of it in terms that a whale would understand. "It's like the best food you've ever tasted, with more of the best stuff you've ever tasted on top of it, with another best food sprinkled on top."

"Like mackerel with krill and then plankton on top?" Meg sang happily.

"No," I said, not holding back a disgusted face. Meg wouldn't be able to see my face anyway. Those fish stacked on each other were nothing like a cookie. If Marc asked if I wanted to go eat mackerel with krill I think that might have made our friendship worse. But Meg did have the right idea for her. "Well, maybe it would be like that for you, I guess."

"And yesterday I got one of my mom's old journals. I've been reading it just a little at a time. I don't want to go through it too fast." And I didn't. I wouldn't. It was like my mom was talking to me. She talked about my first steps and everyone supporting me. I loved it. I'd learned a lot since then.

I kicked at a little collection of pebbles on the beach. "But also, yesterday, my dad found out that I talk to you and he thinks I'm making it up. That it's pretend." I hated that. It didn't feel like Dad was behind me.

"He does?" Meg seemed surprised, but then changed her tone. "Actually, that makes sense. Other whales would think I'm making it up too."

I grimaced. "I know. But I *can* talk to you. I can. And now he's worried I might be a little more," it was hard to say, ". . . broken than he thought."

"Oh, dear. Are you?" Meg asked.

"Maybe a little," I said. Then I realized that Meg probably pictured something like a piece of coral breaking off. "I mean, I'm not *really* broken. It's not like my heart is actually cracked. But I still get really sad and I might need extra help." I waited a moment. "But I don't want them to tell me to stop talking to you. I like talking to you."

"I like it too," Meg said.

"But if I have to go to a therapist, people might find out I'm broken. And that might ruin everything with Marc," I said, scooping up a handful of pebbles.

"A therapist?" Meg asked.

I started picking out the white rocks from my palm. "It's a person that you talk to who helps you with your problems."

"Why would people not like it if you were getting better?" Meg asked.

I opened my mouth to answer, but didn't have anything to say. I picked out a few more white pebbles, then threw them back into the ocean.

"I've heard," Meg said, "that in the Antarctic there are penguins." She paused. "Do you know what a penguin is?"

"Yes," The question felt odd. Everyone knew what a penguin was. I bet even Hannah could point one out.

"Wonderful," Meg said. "I didn't. A friend had to explain them to me. I don't migrate south enough to see them. And you can't find them up north anywhere." She let out a musical sigh. "Where was I? Oh, right. The dad penguin is in charge of the egg for two cold months while the mother treks to the ocean to hunt. He sits on the egg to keep it warm and because he needs to stay with the egg he gets so very hungry. But still, he doesn't abandon his child. The whale who told me the story said that these dads can get so hungry waiting that they can be half their weight by the time the mother returns with food."

"Those are really good dads," I said, trying to guess the moral of this story.

"Yes, indeed," Meg said, then added, "Why was I telling you this story?"

"Because I have a good dad too?"

Meg laughed. "Oh, yes, you do. You really do. But I wanted you to see that sometimes we are all like that egg. And we need help. That egg couldn't keep itself warm. That egg couldn't go hunting. It needs its father. It's not bad to need help sometimes."

That sounded like something my dad would say, except without the penguins. He had tried to explain to me that going to a therapist shouldn't be any more embarrassing than seeing a dentist when you have a toothache. That seeing a therapist when you needed to was actually the smart thing to do. It would be foolish not to take care of a broken arm. And it would be foolish not to see a therapist when you really needed one. If someone's emotions are hurt badly, the wise thing to do is to get help. He even said that he went to a therapist right after the divorce.

Maybe my dad and Meg were right. I'd think about it some more.

"I need help with something else right now," I said, running my hand over the rough rock of the tide pool while the spray misted me. "The people around here don't know what to do with Blue. There are rumors that they want to cut him up or even explode him. I don't like it."

Meg made a disapproving sound. "I don't like that either," she said. "Is there anything we can do to change that?"

"I don't know," I said. "I'm really thinking about it."

"You have a big heart, Willa," Meg said. "That's one thing that tragedy can do for people. When someone loses their mother, they have a bigger heart toward someone else who loses someone."

Maybe that was true. I did feel really strongly about this. "But," I said, "if we were to measure hearts, yours is definitely bigger."

"True," Meg said with a sing-songy laugh. Hers was probably bigger than my entire chest. "In size. But I really like yours."

"Thanks," I said, "but what can I do for Blue? How do I give him a respectful goodbye?"

Meg thought for a moment. "For humpbacks, we stay by our loved one while they float. And when they fall, we say goodbye and move on."

I had to think about that for a moment, picture it. "I like that idea," I said. I wished Blue could be in the ocean surrounded by his family, and then they could move on once he sank. It would be like a whale underwater funeral. "But I don't think that's going to work. He's stranded here; we don't have a way to get him far enough into the ocean." I had to think of something else.

"Hmmm," Meg thought. "I'm not very familiar with what you do on land. Could you get your pod together to do something for him?"

Me and my pod?

I started to think about that, and then I had an idea.

CHAPTER 34

Like You

Maylan Twitchell, Journal
#13, twelve years ago

I saw three specimens of <u>Oxycomanthus Bennetti</u> feather stars on this afternoon's dive. One of them was swimming, which is still one of the most entrancing things to see in all the ocean. It was beautiful, with Key lime and neon yellow legs, flipping over and over each other, like a swimming spider. This one had close to forty or fifty legs moving in a synchronization that was completely hypnotizing.

It's funny to think that less than 200 years ago we thought that these were stationary plants, and then when we figured out that they were animals in the 1800s, we still only believed that they crawled along the bottom of the sea bed. But science was wrong again. They move like nothing else on this planet. We have to be careful about being too sure that we're right sometimes.

~~~~~~~~~~~~~~~~

"So we've got some ideas, but it's still not enough," I said, my legs pushing hard against the pedals. It had been a few days. Blue was stinkier. The crowds came and went. And I had asked my dad for help. That was hard after he said I should think about seeing a therapist. But I asked, and he helped. He had some breakthrough ideas and was emailing and calling people about them. I hoped his ideas worked. But even if they did, it wouldn't completely solve the problem. We asked Jean, and she had some helpful connections, too.

"I know," Marc said, riding his bike beside me. "But I think we're on the right trail." His family was also thinking of ways to help Blue.

As I glanced over at my friend, I noticed that he was a little different—a little happier. He still hadn't told me what had been bothering him. I guess it was too much for now. But ever since we chatted over cookies, we spoke more often. And it wasn't just about my mom, or this meeting with the city. We just talked.

Except about the exploding whale video. I didn't want to talk about that.

I had asked my pod for help. Good move. But right now, I was glad that I asked Marc if there was any way we could get back to swim team. And though he was nervous, he agreed to ask his parents for the money. He didn't tell me why that was hard, but he did it. And they surprised him. They didn't know he was going to swim team and despite whatever problem they were having, they agreed to pay.

He was still worried about the money, but we were headed back to the community pool.

"Maybe we should ask Mr. Norton," I said, still pedaling. "He might be able to help."

"And," Marc said, "we could ask one of the other smartest people I know."

"Perfect," I said. "Who?"

He smiled a dolphin-like mischievous smile. "Lizzy Wallace."

I glared at him.

"No way," I said, pumping my pedals a little harder. "She's the worst." Like a barnacle clinging to my boat.

"Nope," Marc said. "Lex Luthor is the worst. Hitler is the worst. ET on Atari was the worst. Lizzy is just a smart girl."

I liked the idea of comparing her to a supervillain or a horrible video game. "She's always trying to show off how much better she is at everything. And then she rubs my face in it. Grades, debate, swim. Anytime she can."

"Lizzy?" Marc asked. He was panting a little. We had to ride up a hill to get to the community center. "She isn't mean," he said. "Sure, she's smart and is always trying to get attention for it. And maybe she does some awkward stuff, but she isn't mean." He pedaled a few more times. "At least I don't think she's trying to be."

"Are you kidding me?" I almost growled out the words as we climbed the hill. "She's my enemy."

"She is not," Marc said. "You don't have an enemy."

"Yes, she is," I said.

"She asks about scores. And she wants to win debates." He panted more as we crested the hill and pulled into the community center parking lot. "In fact, I think in some ways you two are a lot alike."

I almost fell off my bike.

"No," I said, bumping my wheels up the curb and zooming towards the bike rack.

"Yeah," he said. "When she finishes swimming, she looks around to see how she did compared to everyone else. You do the same thing. She cares about test scores a lot. So do you. You've asked me what I got on tests before, too. And you've mentioned what you got, and that was always better than me." I had. I remembered that. But I didn't do it to rub Marc's face in it, like Lizzy did to me. At least, that's not how I meant it. "And when you win something, you look really proud of yourself too. It's not bad. It's just what you and Lizzy do."

I think my mouth fell open, like largemouth-bass open. There was no way he was right. Right?

"What are you guys talking about?" a voice asked by the entrance. We turned and Lizzy was holding the door open. And she looked just as super confident and annoying as ever.

"Just stuff," Marc said as we walked toward the door. Not a brilliant cover, but it would do.

"It's good to see you," she said. "We missed you last practice." And she did one of her annoying, I'm-better-than-you smiles. "But I warn you, I got faster while you guys have been gone." Yep.

Same Lizzy. Now she could feel better about herself because I was back to being the slow one.

But as I walked past her, I wondered if maybe it was just a normal smile—not a fake I'm-better-than-you smile. And maybe she just wanted attention. That wasn't the same as being mean. It's possible she needed it bad enough that she didn't notice that it could make other people feel bad.

Maybe it was just how she tried to get through middle school. Maybe.

And maybe I would ask for her help.

CHAPTER 35

City Council

Maylan Twitchell, Journal #13,
twelve years ago

Migration means different things to different animals.

Creatures in the mesopelagic zone travel from the dark deep to the surface every evening, looking for a meal or favorable temperatures, and then make their way back down every morning. A daily migration.

Whales, to the best of our knowledge, migrate every year from the cold waters to the warm waters and back again. An annual migration.

The bluefish tuna is born off the coast of Japan and swims to California, 5,000 miles, when it is still very young. There it will spend several years growing, then return all of the way back to Japan to spawn. A life migration.

All of these creatures know better than to just stay where they are. They need to be on the move. They have somewhere they're supposed to be.

And if they are going to make a terrifying, dangerous, amazing journey, isn't it great that they've got schools and pods and families to help them out?

The city council room was underwhelming to say the least. I was expecting at least dark solid wood desks that looked like a courtroom, or maybe an ornate podium. Nope. Instead, the Tupkuk Island City Council, all five of them, met in the back of the city building in a multipurpose room. There was a portable basketball hoop pushed up against the wall and thin, worn carpet on the floor. We all were seated in metal folding chairs and there wasn't enough room for everyone to sit. People lined the back and were even standing in the hall outside the door. It was probably a record attendance, but for such a small room that wasn't very many.

My dad sat beside me, nervously playing with his beard. He'd even bought a new suit. He didn't have to come. I could have ridden my bike here all by myself. Of course, that would have been hard in a dress. I learned that trick from Lizzy. The dress might just make me seem more confident, more professional. I had given my presentation in front of my dad several times now, but he seemed more nervous than I was.

Still, I was glad he was here. And surrounding us was the rest of my pod. All my stepsibs were dressed up nice and sitting by us. Except Masha, who was standing in the doorway, bouncing baby

Hannah. She was dressed in a nice red dress and smiled at me when I turned to look at her.

Papá Mendoza sat behind my family and gave me a thumbs up. Mamá Mendoza whipped her finger, as if to tell me to whip them into shape. I laughed. And Marc nodded.

Maybe everything hadn't worked out perfect in my life, but I did have some great people behind me.

The mayor spoke into a little microphone that broadcast his deep voice throughout the room, "The city now opens the floor on the subject of the dead blue whale in the Lakeside district." He didn't need a microphone; the city council room wasn't that big. Maybe the mic made them feel important.

I didn't want to get out of my seat. I wanted to sit down and let other people do this. Maybe they would have great ideas. Maybe they would take care of this. But I had to be brave. I wasn't sure that anyone cared like I did, or had planned like me and my pod. And Dad said I had something worth sharing.

I stood quickly before my courage swam away like a scared herring, and approached the microphone on the stand for commenters. Again, the room was small, but I was glad I wouldn't have to worry about volume. My message would get across.

Memories of losing my debate to Lizzy came flooding back. I thought I had been prepared then, too, and had lost big time. I took a deep breath. This time would be different. Very different.

At least I hoped it would be.

I cleared my throat. "My name is Willa Twitchell. I live in the Lakeside district," I said. "And I have some ideas about what to do with the whale."

The mayor nodded. He looked at me like I was just being cute. One of the councilmen didn't even raise his eyes to see me, like I was a waste of time. And then there were all the others on the city council and the audience behind me too. Maybe they felt the same way. I hoped to prove that I was worth listening to. "I've heard lots of rumors about what to do, everything from cutting the whale into pieces and burying it, to exploding it, hoping to completely annihilate it, to just letting it rot. I think we can do better than that. I think we need to." Inside, I thought about Blue's pod singing for him.

This would be my song for him.

Because honestly, he wouldn't want me to *actually* sing for him. I'm really, really, really bad.

I looked at the mayor and he wasn't yawning. So far so good. I wasn't super polished or anything, but I didn't sound frightened.

"I found the whale on the beach and tried desperately to keep it alive. I kept it wet, I called emergency services, I gathered people to help me. We did everything that we could, but we couldn't save him." I let out a bunch of air. I wondered if any feeling was coming across with my words. I hoped so. "And somehow when it died, I hurt. It probably had more to do with the fact that my mom died about two months ago, and she loved—" my voice caught inside, but I inhaled slowly and continued, "—she loved every creature in the ocean. And she taught me to as well. This whale isn't just a nuisance to be disposed of. This whale had a pod, and judging by his age, children. This whale didn't just come out of nowhere. This whale has lived a life, longer than me, longer than a lot of people in this room. And he was rare and endangered. I think he deserves to be treated with respect as we decide what to do here today." The mayor leaned forward and the councilman who was ignoring me looked up.

"I'm going to suggest a few things. And I had a lot of help coming up with them." I looked back at my pod.

"My dad had a great idea. You see, my mom was a marine biologist at Northwest Washington University." I didn't stumble this time when I talked about her. "And he wondered if they wouldn't be interested in this whale for their marine biology department. He called them and talked to them several times, pitching his idea for them to take the whale." I remember hearing a few of these conversations as most of them were video calls. The men and women there spoke so highly of my mother it brought back stings—and also immense pride. "They expressed interest, but were concerned with the logistics of transporting it." Lizzy gave me that sentence. "They had grant money that they could apply to the effort, but it wouldn't cover it all. So," I raised a finger, "we had one important part of a solution." I noticed all of the council was looking at me now.

"Then I asked my friend Jean Lambert. She has a nephew with a construction company in Oregon and that nephew has a friend with a construction company in Seattle. That company said they would donate three days use of their equipment and a few of their men to move the whale. An incredible donation that would take care of more costs."

"We knew we would need water transport for the equipment and for the whale, and who better than our local Juan Mendoza?" I turned and gestured toward Papá Mendoza as he raised his hand to receive the praise. It made me smile. I know where Marc gets his goofy bravado. "He said that he had connections to a boat that would be big enough for both jobs. He is trading labor for the use of that boat." I watched as the city council members started to take some notes. I thought that was good, but I wasn't sure.

"But we still didn't have enough money to finish the job," I continued. "Close, but not there yet. That's where my friend Lizzy Wallace comes in." She sat in front of my dad and beamed. "It's expensive to haul and preserve the skeleton of a whale like this. I talked to someone who might just be smarter than me. She did a lot of research and found out that there are organizations across the country that have money to donate for marine life education. She has contacted several of them, and we have covered almost all of our other costs. And we might have some pledges for more still coming." Her parents may have helped her, but I figured that I would give her all the attention for this. She might need it.

The mayor scribbled down more notes.

"Even my stepmom helped out by setting up a social media funding page and linking it to a video channel where I posted my pictures and videos of ocean creatures." I almost hadn't talked to Masha about this, but I was glad I did. She was a pretty smart lady when it came to social media marketing. "A video I posted of a humpback whale breaching only a few yards from me already has enough views that we should be able to pay for the truck driver. If this trend continues, we should be able to finish covering the costs with nothing asked of the city whatsoever."

Caleb gave his mom two thumbs up, clearly proud of her contribution.

"And last but not least, my seven-year-old stepbrother gave me this five-dollar bill that he has been saving since his birthday." I pulled the bill from my pocket. Yes, my dress was that awesome. "It was all the money that he had, but he wanted to help." He had overheard me talking about it with Masha and he offered. Super sweet. I needed to get to know that kid better. Masha gave Caleb two thumbs up and he looked pretty proud of himself.

"That's my proposal," I said, shifting to squarely face the mayor and the council. "You will find more thorough information in your email inboxes if you would like some time to look it over. And you are welcome to ask me, or my pod—" I quickly corrected myself, "—or my team any questions you might have. Thank you."

I almost curtseyed like Lizzy had at the end of her debate, but I didn't. I gave kind of a half nod.

Before I could turn to go back to my seat, someone clapped. I couldn't tell who it was. Maybe it was my dad or Marc. But someone else joined. And then someone else. When I looked behind me, they all were clapping. I don't know why. Maybe they weren't expecting a presentation like this. Maybe they were expecting something else.

The mayor clapped too, then leaned forward.

He looked at me, this time almost like he was asking permission to speak. I nodded. "That is quite the amazing presentation," he said. "Maybe we should have you come work for the city in a few years." A lot of people laughed at that. But it was a good laugh. Like he was right.

He wasn't. That job would make me nutty. It didn't have anything to do with the ocean.

The mayor addressed the whole room. "Would anyone else like to give us a proposal or voice their concern?" He surveyed the room. It was quiet until Mr. Ford, the owner of the country club, said, "As long as we're not blowing it up or letting it rot downwind of my golf course, I'm good."

Everyone laughed again. The mayor took a second to look around the room, but no one spoke or raised their hand. "Well, then," the mayor said, "would anyone object if we forward Willa Twitchell's plan to the state wildlife department as our city's recommendation for what should happen with this blue whale?" The mayor once again surveyed the room. And then he struck his gavel on the table. "No objections. This meeting is adjourned."

CHAPTER 36

Hard to Say

Maylan Twitchell, Journal #13,
twelve years ago

The first time I saw a moray eel, I thought it was going to bite me. I was young, snorkeling in Mexico and I came upon it by accident. It closed and opened its mouth, showing me its sharp teeth, threatening me to back off and I got the message loud and clear.

It was later that I learned that opening and closing its mouth like that was just how moray eels breathe. Though you should always give them their space (those teeth are sharp!), that eel wasn't trying to scare me. It was just watching me like I was watching it.

I learned a lesson that day not to jump to conclusions. In my job we observe, observe, and observe. Then we give it our best guess.

The large metal arms of two huge cranes extended out over my cove. Their massive steel lifting cables descended all the way down to Blue.

It had taken over a week for all of the proper paperwork to go through and to coordinate the truck. But on a bright and sunny Saturday morning, right after the fog burned away, a huge semitruck sat on the highway with traffic being directed around it.

Construction workers stood around Blue's body, setting up the cables that dangled from the cranes. It probably wasn't a very pleasant job. He had been dead for a while, but was still in decent shape. Of course, he didn't smell very good. I couldn't imagine how they were going to lift him. I was never meant to be an engineer.

"This just might work," Marc said. A large crowd had come out to watch, but Marc and I had climbed a ridge to one side of the cove. We had a great view and the space to ourselves.

"After all our hard work, it'd better," I said.

It was going to take a while to get Blue all attached. So we talked. We talked about school, swim team, and about how Hannah was starting to walk. I even told him about my therapist and how she was helping me. I was really nervous that he would think that was weird or something, but he seemed pretty chill about the whole thing.

Marc got quiet for a while, then spoke softer. "So," he said, "you said that you're my friend no matter what, right?"

"Definitely," I said.

"Remember how you talked about your mom when we got cookies? You shared what was really bothering you?"

"Yeah," I said, looking back at Marc instead of at the huge cranes.

"And I said that maybe some time I could tell you what's really been bugging me?"

"Yeah."

"Those words have haunted me," he said. "I knew that some time I'd need to tell you." He blew out a bunch of air. "And this is going to be hard to say." He wasn't smiling. He ran his fingers through his hair, and some strands stood up. He looked like a nervous roosterfish.

He pounded his own fist once. "Really hard to say."

I wanted to encourage him, tell him it was okay to talk, but I just waited.

"Now, you can't overreact, okay?" he said, pointing at me.

I nodded.

"And you won't think my family is terrible or anything?"

I shook my head. "I know you guys too well." But the fact that he asked made me really nervous. What was he going to tell me?

Marc puffed up his cheeks, then he looked like he was going to say something, but didn't. Then he did it again. Finally, he started talking again. "It's just . . . she . . . I . . . didn't." It just wasn't coming out. Then the tears started. I had never seen Marc cry.

He wiped them away quickly and blinked to keep them from returning. "Sofia is—" he started, but then stopped again. "She's—" And he still couldn't say it. He took a deep breath. "She's not learning like you think."

"Okay," I said.

"She's in a hospital," Marc said.

"Yeah," I said. "Your mom said that." Was she not studying health? Was she sick herself? Like sick so bad she was in a hospital for months?

Marc shook his head. "No. It's more of a clinic. And the only learning she's doing is learning to get off drugs." He paused. "She's addicted to a lot of them. And she's in the hospital full-time trying to get off them." His brows dipped and he squeezed his eyes shut in a struggle to hold back tears.

Addicted to drugs. I would have never guessed. What was that like to have a sister going through that?

"It got really bad," he said, more tears streaming. "She started more than a year ago, but it got so bad that she was stealing from us. I had saved fifty dollars to buy the next *Call to Action* game when it came out, but one day the money was gone—disap-peared. It had taken me three months to save that money. And she stole it. I was so mad at her." He shook his head. "I mean, like completely furious. Plus, she stole so much more from my parents. And from other people too.

"We tried to help her on our own, but she had gotten angry and mean. She didn't want our help. It was tearing up my parents' hearts and I hated her for it." Marc punched his own fist again. "Eventually, it got so bad that my parents took her to the rehab clinic. She won't talk to us. She's furious. And it's expensive, really expensive. She's had to do it a few times. Between that and paying back all the money she stole, my parents decided to move into the marina—to save money to pay for everything."

"That's why you didn't think you could do swim team?"

"Yeah," he nodded, "but my parents said that just because

they were spending a lot on my sister didn't mean they didn't have any left for me and Dante." He sniffled. "It just felt like that, so I thought it was true." He lifted his chin and took a deep breath. "She went from being fun and a great sister to being someone I didn't even know."

He kicked his legs a little. "I just want her back."

There was a pause so I spoke. "I'm sorry. I really like Sofia. She's a good person."

"I think that's what's so embarrassing about it," Marc said. "She was a good person. We have a good family. We come from a good heritage, a good culture. What will people say if they find out about her?"

A gull landed right next to us and we watched it pace the ground. "I don't know," I said. "I'd hope they'd just want to help." I put my hand on his shoulder. I wanted to hug him, but I didn't know if that would help or hurt. So I did what he'd done for me. "Thanks for telling me," I said. "That's got to be really hard."

Marc nodded. And then we talked more. We stared at the huge cranes getting a massive dead whale ready to be moved and we talked. My mom was gone. And a beautiful blue whale was gone too. And my best friend was terrified that his sister was gone. That he wouldn't get her back.

Finally, we watched the cranes lift Blue slowly all the way up out of the cove, and then lower him onto the two trailers of the ginormous truck. He fit. Not perfectly, but he fit. After Mrs. Ingebretsen snapped a few pictures for the newspaper, the semi slowly started down the highway until we couldn't see it anymore.

And Marc and I talked some more.

CHAPTER 37

On the Blocks

Maylan Twitchell, Journal #13,
twelve years ago

In grad school I learned that there are twenty million tons of gold in the ocean. It's right under our noses. But seeing it is nearly impossible because it's dissolved. It's one of the minerals found in the water. The trick is realizing that it's there and recognizing that the ocean is incredibly valuable.

Sometimes I see my little girl and hope others can find the gold in her. But more importantly, I hope she can see the gold in herself.

A whole line of swimmers stood on their blocks.

We raced in heats. Only eight people could race at a time, so a group of eight would line up and race. Then another.

It was the Tupkuk Tornadoes against the Oceanview Tiger

Sharks. For a swim team, Tiger Sharks is a much better name than Tornadoes. Well, kind of. Tiger Sharks sounds cool, but they don't actually swim that fast. Usually only about two and a half miles per hour. They can do some crazy bursts of speed, but only for a few seconds. They're kind of like tigers in the zoo. They are capable of moving really fast, but most of the time, they just laze around.

But these Tiger Sharks weren't lazy.

The bald official with the whistle called out, "Step up. Take your mark." The man wore a jacket that was too big for him. Or maybe his head was just a little too small for the rest of his body. Either way he looked a little like a turtle. He blew his whistle.

I wasn't on the blocks yet. It wasn't my turn. But my heart thudded like it was.

At the sound of the whistle, Marc leapt off his blocks.

"Go, Marc!" I screamed and clapped. I'm sure he heard it before he clumsily crashed into the water. He definitely didn't have the dive down yet. That started him off near last place.

"*Vamos*, Marc! *Vamos! Vamos!*" Mamá Mendoza screamed from the bleachers for him to go, go, go. Papá Mendoza and Dante screamed too. My family was also there cheering.

"Go, Marc!" It was Lizzy. She stood next to me, her suit and swim cap matching like she was a pro. And she was stretching while she cheered.

She still kind of bugged me, but not as bad as before. I mean, I think I understood her a little bit.

Marc surfaced from the water and what he didn't have in form and style, he made up for in intensity. He smashed that water and pushed himself through.

I hadn't really just watched him swim before. We were usually swimming at the same time and I was behind him. But as I watched, I was impressed.

I screamed again. So did Lizzy.

Our cheers calmed a little as all the swimmers got into their pace.

"Hey," I said, glancing over at Lizzy between claps, "thanks again for all that help you gave me with the blue whale." It felt weird to voluntarily talk to Lizzy Wallace, let alone thank her.

"My pleasure," she said, stretching again. "I already told you that." She still said everything like she was better than me.

I didn't let it get to me. At least, not as much as before.

Was Marc right that I was kind of like Lizzy? Did I do stuff like that?

Marc caught up to one of the two swimmers in front of him. I cheered again. I knew he probably couldn't hear me with all the water sloshing through his ears, but he was doing great.

"You've got this," Lizzy called out, even a little louder than I did. She wasn't stretching any more.

Marc kept gaining. He caught the next swimmer. Then passed. Both Lizzy and I were screaming and jumping up and down. A lot of the rest of the team was too. I didn't know if this was what you did at a swim meet or not, but I couldn't help it.

Marc crashed forward like he was being chased by a hammerhead shark.

Or like he needed this.

There were only like thirty feet left in the race. And Marc

kicked it in even faster. I guess he had more inside him. He started to gain on the boy who was winning.

Our cheering grew even more frantic.

And then Marc pushed forward even faster. It was like he had a motor. He was the motor. In the last few yards, he passed the leader and beat him by an arm's length.

Our whole team went crazy. From last to first place. I turned and gave Lizzy a high ten. Then she hugged me. I hugged her back.

"That was amazing," I screamed at Marc as he was getting out of the water. His smile somehow seemed wider than his face.

"Incredible," Lizzy said. And he approached both of us and gave us high fives. He still hadn't dried himself off all the way, so water splashed in our faces.

I would definitely have to include this in my journal.

"Your turn," he said to Lizzy.

And it was.

"Okay," she said. And took a deep breath. "Wish me luck."

I did.

She exhaled big and for the first time, I realized she was nervous. Just like I was going to be when it was my turn.

While she was on the block, she even looked over a couple of times at us. She still did all her professional-looking stretches and stood tall and confident, but it was like she really wanted us to cheer her on. And like she hoped she didn't mess up for us. I didn't know if I just hadn't seen it before, but she wanted support. At least here she didn't seem like she had it all under control.

She double-checked to make sure all her hair was tucked under her cap, and checked her goggles like TV cameras were filming her and she was starting some huge race with commentators talking about her every move.

But that was just so Lizzy. She might be more quirky than snobby. And she didn't annoy me as much anymore.

"Go, Lizzy!" I said, almost not even realizing.

She smiled from the blocks and nodded. And I didn't think it was fake.

When the turtle man started her race, she rocketed off the blocks in total grace. It was like she could fly for a second. And when she came up, she swam with perfect strokes. She probably had practiced until she mastered it. But she wasn't as aggressive as Marc and she had competition.

Marc and I both cheered her on through the end of the race. To the very end. She got second.

And then I felt this strange feeling. I was sad she hadn't won. I don't know if it was because we were on the same team now, or what. Maybe something had changed.

"Good job," I said as she came out of the water. I gave her a high ten. Marc did too.

"Sorry, guys," she said. "I'll do better in my freestyle relay." She dried off her face. "Now you're up," she said, looking at me.

And I think my heart totally stopped cold.

I was in the next heat.

CHAPTER 38

Finally Winning

Maylan Twitchell, Journal #13,
twelve years ago

Weighing in at the size of an African elephant, the mola mola fish is the biggest boney fish in the sea. They can grow to several times larger than a human, but look flat and awkward, with large, unblinking eyes. Because of their appearance, their slow movement, their curious and unfearful nature, and some lazy-looking behavior, the poor mola mola is often referred to as the stupidest fish in the sea.

But that's unfair. Being gentle is not the same as being stupid.

~~~~~~~~~~~~~~~~~~~~

As I stood on the blocks, I was a few seconds away from an anxiety attack. My heart pounded like the waves against the rocks.

What was I thinking?

At least the crowd wasn't huge, just pockets of people scattered throughout the bleachers. They were all parents and family members of everyone about to swim in our first swim meet ever. But it made me really nervous anyway.

The girl next to me had to be five inches taller and in a lot better shape. I felt silly even standing next to her.

"Alright, Willa," someone yelled. "*Vamos!*" I looked up to see Mamá Mendoza clapping and yelling.

"Go, Willa," my dad called out. Masha whistled loud and Nadia, unsuccessfully, tried to copy her. I heard Caleb too. I don't know if they were all excited to be here, but I really appreciated it. It didn't fill the giant hole in me, that was my mom's—but it filled up some cracks.

This was happening. My first race. But I probably wasn't going to do very well; I couldn't even win against my own team. How would I beat anyone else from the other team? I felt a bit embarrassed already.

"Willa, Willa," Marc chanted. Then Lizzy and some of the other members of the team joined in.

I couldn't help but smile. Which was really dangerous when I was about to jump into the water.

"Take your mark," the bald man with the turtle head said. Then he blew his whistle.

I leapt in, like a stingray gliding back into the ocean after it shot out of the water. No one really knows why they leap out, but they slap the water when they come back in. That's what I did.

And then, stroke for stroke, I pushed myself. I tried to

imagine a sailfish or marlin or something else super speedy. I wanted the grace of Lizzy, but the intensity of Marc. But I knew I wasn't going to win.

As I came up for air, I heard "Willa. Willa." And I found a little more in me.

I just kept going and going.

I needed to breathe but I didn't dare surface for air. It was only a stroke or two and I'd be done.

When my hand hit the end of the pool my head shot straight out and I gasped. I did it. I finished my first swim race.

I looked around and realized I came in dead last. One of the girls wasn't even in the water anymore.

Last.

I laughed because I felt like I had two choices, laugh or cry, and I had already done more than enough crying.

Somebody whistled through their fingers. Happy whistles. "Good job, Willa. Good job!" My dad. Lumberjack cheers from the crowd.

"Good job?" A kid's voice asked. "She was the very last one." Caleb. Despite all the echoing sounds in the room, I could hear him. I guess he didn't understand what Dad was trying to do.

But in the next heat, I was second to last. And in the next. On my last race, I was third to last.

Progress.

Or the kids I swam against were younger.

In the end, I didn't hate it.

Coach Jackson had us all line up before we went home. "Good job today, everyone," Coach said, looking down at her clipboard then back up at us. For some reason she had a paper sack next to her. "So you've had your first swim meet. What did you think?"

Lizzy's arm shot up. No surprise. "I really liked competing," she said. "It felt different than just swimming against each other."

I thought the same thing, but now I didn't want to say it, even if Lizzy was okay now.

"I thought it was different to have an official," Skyler, the red-headed kid said. He was a grade above me and did quite well in the meet. "And did anyone else think he kind of looked like he had a turtle head?"

Everyone broke out in a quick laugh.

"Be respectful," chastised Coach Jackson, but smiled a little too. "I've been timing you and watching your progress and I have a few pointers about how you can prepare and be even more ready for your next meet." She took a few steps down the line. "But we'll save those for practice."

"And," she said, "I don't want to focus so much about what we can still do better that I don't recognize all the good work you've done." I liked the sound of that. "I have two awards today," she said and grabbed the brown paper sack she had next to her. "It isn't much," she said. "Just a certificate and a candy bar, but it's important to recognize what we've done well. And I feel a few of you deserve some special recognition."

I looked down the line of us. Everyone was fixed on Coach Jackson. I think Lizzy was standing especially tall.

"The first honor," Coach Jackson said, "goes to our top swimmer at the meet. He won two races and came in second on the other two. And he did it all while still learning how to dive." Coach Jackson smiled big and we all knew who it was. His dives looked like long-legged belly-flops. She pulled out the certificate and the candy bar. He had even beat out Claire, the sandy-haired girl who had started out the fastest on the team. "Marc Mendoza." Everyone clapped. Especially me. Even though it was really embarrassing for me to lose over and over again, maybe it was worth it just to be here for my friend.

Marc walked forward and shyly accepted his award. "One thing I want to point out about Marc is his effort, his heart," Coach Jackson said. "Though he is still working on his mechanics, his sheer effort is helping him achieve. Imagine what he'll be like when he gets the mechanics down."

He blushed. I'm not sure if it was because he was just complimented, or told he had something to work on. Still, I was proud of him.

"And for the other award," Coach Jackson said. It had to be for Lizzy or Claire. They were the next best swimmers. "Willa Twitchell."

"Me?" That didn't make any sense. I'd lost every race.

"Yes, you," Coach Jackson said. I'm sure my surprise was all over my face. Maybe the others looked surprised too because Coach Jackson had a few things to say. "Did you all know that Willa has dropped several seconds each time she has raced? *Several seconds,*" she repeated a little louder. "From her beginning trial run until now, which was only a few weeks ago, she has dropped nearly twenty seconds. That's a *huge* improvement." She walked back and forth. "Do you remember how I told you that I was the seventeenth fastest swimmer in the world?" We all nodded. "And that I only lost to the best swimmer by four seconds?" She let that sink in. "Think of how much difference twenty seconds makes." She paused. "*Twenty seconds*," she repeated. "If Willa were to continue improving at this rate, she would break the world record within the year."

Whoa. I had never thought of that.

"Now, it's going to get harder and harder to improve," Coach Jackson said. "It always does. But . . ." She looked at each person on the swim team. "I'm going to challenge you all to be like Willa, to improve. To get better. Be faster than you were. Try harder. That's what swimming is all about."

And then Coach Jackson reached into the bag and gave me a certificate and a Snickers bar.

Maybe Coach Jackson never won a gold. Maybe she was only the seventeenth fastest swimmer in the world. But right then, she was definitely my favorite swimmer ever.

I thought I would keep that certificate for forever. But I would definitely eat the Snickers. And hopefully I would do what she said; just keep trying and improving.

CHAPTER 39

Migration

Maylan Twitchell, Journal #13, twelve years ago

The ocean is always moving. There are surface currents and eddies. Upwellings are places where deep water comes to the surface. In downwellings, surface water sinks. Waves and tides are never still. If you lose your hat, it might end up on the other side of the world. The perpetual motion of it all is mesmerizing, always moving, always changing.

Sometimes life is like that too.

〰〰〰〰〰〰〰〰〰

I drew a humpback in my journal while I caught Meg up on everything that had happened.

"So you're saying Lizzy isn't an evil bottom dweller anymore?" Meg asked.

I closed my journal. "I don't think so. I think she just needs attention."

"Hmmm," Meg hummed while she thought. "That's not all bad. I like attention too." And then out in the distance I saw a large whale rise out of the water to do a backflop. It was probably half a mile away.

"Meg," I said. "Was that you? I just saw the most amazing humpback shoot out of the water."

She giggled a song. "Amazing humpback," she repeated. "I love a pleasant surprise."

"You're right there." I pointed, still stunned. I always thought of her as being miles away, sending her song through the water. "Close enough for me to see you."

"All amazing 66,000 pounds of me," Meg said, and she surfaced again with a slap. Yeah, she definitely wasn't self-conscious about her weight. I could imagine her wide smile as she started to swim toward me.

"Don't get too close," I said. I didn't want her to get beached.

"I won't," she said. "I just wanted to look at you again, my favorite little human, not just hear you." And I saw her poke her head out of the water and spyhop so she could see me.

I stood up and waved my arms.

For a moment, we just looked at each other.

"Thank you for being my friend, Willa," Meg sang.

"Thank you for being *my* friend," I said. The idea of being friends with a humpback whale basically fulfilled my every dream. So why did I feel a little sad?

Meg paused. "This might be hard to hear," she said. "It's hard to say." I didn't like the sound of that. And then Meg said words I definitely didn't like. "It's time for me to migrate north."

My insides whirlpooled. Migration. Meg was leaving, swimming thousands of miles away. No more talks. No more call-outs or compliments. No more stories. No more Meg.

There was no avoiding it. She was always going to do it.

But I wasn't ready.

"It's time to go with my pod, my friends, my family," Meg said. "There is great krill up there and the adventure is good for me."

Was this how my life was going to be? Meeting and making friends and then having to let them go?

"Are you coming back?" I asked. I think my words came out a little softer than I meant.

"Always." Meg did that bubble laugh that I hadn't heard her do for a while. I gave a small smile in spite of myself. "When the weather gets cold there, I will come back here. When the weather gets cold here, then I will go further south. It's what I do."

She was right. There was no keeping her here. Mom was right. Life was always moving.

"But before I go, can I tell you a story?" Meg asked.

"Of course." I sat down. These stories usually required my whole brain to understand.

"I told you that I've had a few children. Well, when I had my first calf, she meant the world to me. We would swim and whisper, whisper and giggle, eat and swim, and swim some more. She was smart and fast. In the murky water we would have to stay in constant communication so I would know where she was. But it was scary because even though we were careful and quiet, if a predator heard us, things could change fast. So I did my very best to steer her around trouble and keep quiet. It was scary being a new mother. I had never done this before. I could tell you a dozen times when I messed up. But my daughter stuck right by me . . ."

That would definitely be scary to raise a calf in the ocean.

". . . until she was grown," Meg said. "And she grew up to be smart and fast. And then it was time for her to leave, to live her own life." She exhaled long. "It was normal for her to leave. It was time for her to strike out into the deep ocean, have an adventure, to grow even more, maybe even become a mother herself."

That made sense.

"It's a big ocean, so I don't see her as much as I want," Meg said. "In fact, I rarely see her. But I will never stop thinking about her. Ever."

The waves came in and out while I thought about those words.

"It's okay that she has moved on," Meg said. "She will always be a part of me."

Another wave came in and out.

Meg waited, like I was supposed to say something.

"It's okay for us to move on," Meg said.

"Okay," I whispered.

"I love you, Willa."

"I love you too," I said.

"You," Meg said, "little human, are my favorite pleasant surprise." Her voice was serious.

Everyone should definitely have their own whale.

"Are you going to be okay while I'm gone?" she asked.

I thought about it for a moment. Everything was still really hard, but I wasn't drowning. My dad had taken me out to dinner. He said we should do that every other week. Just us. So he could pay attention to me and I could talk about whatever I wanted. And it was quiet and nice and not filled with screaming kids. At the end, he set out a few dollars and some coins for the tip. But then he picked a coin up and made it disappear, only to "find" it from behind my ear. Part of me wanted to roll my eyes—I wasn't six anymore—but the rest of me loved it. It was like a part of my old dad was back. He said we could even do another whale watch.

Maybe in a couple of weeks I'd be comfortable enough to tell him to shave his beard.

And Masha. She wasn't taking me out to dinner or anything, and she still didn't like how I made sandwiches when I was hungry, but I asked her what she was always doing on her phone and she showed me. So I sent a friend request and she accepted it on social media. She actually posts some really funny and cool stuff. I mean, it's not like awesome videos of back-flopping humpback whales, but it's fun. A lot of it is just what my stepsibs say and the trouble they get into. I think it's how she deals with it all. I comment sometimes and she always responds. I like it. And for my birthday she posted my picture and said some pretty nice things about me. I think she really likes me.

My stepsibs were still loud and cute—but loud. Did I mention that they were loud? Caleb still hangs out on the front porch, Nadia gets overexcited, Garth always repeats what everyone says, and I still feel like waking Hannah is considered the worst thing

I could possibly do in this house. But they're all pretty fun in their own way. Being part of a big family was never something I think I'd ever choose for myself, but it wasn't as bad as I thought. In fact, once you get used to it, there are some really good things about it.

And Marc and his family. I had dinner over there three times in the last few weeks. I love those people.

Lizzy is still Lizzy. We actually talk quite a bit now, mostly in class and at swim. In front of the whole class, she told Mr. Norton she wanted to be on my debate team, but then no one else in the class would stand a chance. And then Mr. Norton said that she was probably right. I liked that. A lot. He told us that next year we should try out for the school debate team. That didn't seem like a bad idea.

Jean Lambert was always just down the beach. And there was something very comforting about that.

Coach Jackson helped me see how I was getting better.

And I had my therapist for the hard days.

I had a really great pod.

"Yeah," I said back to Meg, "I'll be okay."

Then Meg rose up and did a most spectacular rise and back flop. Just for me.

She told me again she'd miss me. And then she was gone.

The bike ride back home felt heavy, but eventually I made it. I threw my bike in the shed and rushed to the front door. I had told my dad that I'd be back before dinner, and I was cutting it close. Rounding the corner and barreling up the front steps, I toppled over.

Caleb had been sitting on the front steps again.

"Sorry," I said, getting to my feet and making sure he was okay. Thankfully, it was more awkward than painful. "This is a dangerous place to hang out when I'm not looking."

"It's okay," he said, checking his elbow for any scratches.

Weird kid.

I reached for the doorknob, then stopped. "Hey, Caleb," I said, turning and sitting down next to him.

"Yeah?"

"Have you ever been to the tide pools?" I asked, waggling my eyebrows.

He looked intrigued. "What's a tide pool?"

I let out a huge sigh. Who's been training this kid? I sat next to him and pulled out my ocean journal.

CHAPTER 40

Hey, Mom

Willa Twitchell, Journal #5, today

Hey, Mom, I still think about you all the time. More than whales, or feather stars, or crabs, or dolphins. I really miss you. And I always will.

I had to say goodbye to Meg. That was hard. Really hard. Not nearly as bad as saying goodbye to you, but it wasn't easy. You would have liked her. A lot. A ton. All thirty-three tons of her.

The whole family is leaving in a few minutes to go to the university to see Blue. They've got his bones hung from the ceiling and they are having an unveiling. Can you imagine an entire blue whale skeleton displayed across the ceiling of a museum? He probably takes up the whole room. And just seeing him will probably inspire thousands of kids to want to know what happens in the ocean. He was the first blue whale I saw. And he inspired me.

I'm really happy to have been a part of that. That he will be remembered. I'm proud of all of the people that helped.

And Chihiro sent me one of your journals they found in your office. I'm reading it a little at a time. It helps me remember you and how much you love me. She also sent a paper lantern for Obon. She said that during the festival, she'll be dancing to remember you. I'll light the lantern here to remember you, too. To be grateful for you. And so you can find me. I'm not really sure how that works, but I want you to know that someone is definitely thinking about you, during Obon and every day before and after. That someone loves you. That you will never be forgotten.

But before I go see Blue's amazing skeleton, do you remember how you told me that the ocean is filled with more wonders than the most brilliant explorer could ever discover or fully appreciate? And then you said, "Just like you"? And you were pointing to me? I've never forgotten that. And I never will.

And sometimes when I feel sad, really sad, I remember that.

And I choose to believe that you just might be right. I mean, you were a great scientist.

I'll love you forever.

Maylan Twitchell, Journal #13, twelve years ago

I've studied creatures throughout the whole ocean, but none of them are as fascinating as my own baby girl. I love you, Willa. My little human. There are a lot of wonders and beauties in this world that continue to interest and surprise me, and I love a good surprise. But you, Willa, are my favorite pleasant surprise.

Acknowledgments

Hey, you.

Yeah, you.

Thanks for reading this book. Without readers like you there is no reason to write books. Thanks for taking the time and trusting us enough to read *Willa and the Whale*. We hope you liked it. Feel free to hunt us down on social media, or email us at chadcmorris@gmail.com and let us know what you think. We love to hear from readers. And if you liked this book, please spread the word. That's how other amazing readers find their next read. In fact, there's a good chance that you read this book because someone recommended it to you. You can also check out the other books we wrote together, *Mustaches for Maddie* and *Squint*.

If you are a teacher, librarian, media specialist, or administrator, thanks for reading our book, and thanks for all you do that encourages young readers. Your jobs are invaluable. If we can help, let us know. We love to visit schools and do assemblies. We've been all over the nation and have visited hundreds of schools talking about reading, kindness, creativity, friends, and imagination.

And thanks to Shadow Mountain Publishing for publishing this book. Special thanks to Chris Schoebinger, Heidi Taylor, and Lisa Magnum who loved the concept and played important roles in shaping the story. Not only do they help us, but they believe in us, and are our friends. What a publishing company! And thanks to Derk Koldewyn for his editorial eye and hours of help. There would be some pretty embarrassing mistakes without Derk cleaning up our mess. He made our book better. Thanks to Troy Butcher and the marketing team for all of your hard work. Thanks to Emily Remington for the amazing cover. We love it. And thanks to Richard Erickson for the art direction.

Thanks to our agent, Ben Grange, for his advice, help, enthusiasm, cheerleading, etc. He really is the best.

We also need to thank all those who read manuscripts of this book and gave us advice and feedback: Maria Garcia, Susan Allred, Bruce Jacobs, and Josh Hales.

Thanks to all of the marine biologists and enthusiasts out there who write articles and post pictures and videos. We already loved ocean creatures, but we heavily leaned on your expertise and footage. It's absolutely fascinating and you do wonderful work. Seriously, everyone should look up information about Japanese puffer fish, bobbitt worms, humpback whales and any cool creature that catches your attention in this book.

Thanks to everyone who cares about our oceans and all the life in them. They are worth preserving.

Thanks to Melissa Golden and her awesome children who inspired the "get that spatula out of your shirt" line.

To all those who are going through something difficult, let's not be afraid to talk. Talk to a friend, a parent, a therapist, or even a whale. Everyone should have their own whale.

Discussion Questions

1. Willa loves sea creatures. All of them. Even zombie worms. What do you really love? Why?
2. Willa and her mother both kept journals. Have you ever tried to keep a journal before? If you did, what would you write down? Why is it good to have your thoughts and memories written down?
3. Willa's parents went through a divorce, Willa's mother died, and then she had to adjust to a new family. How can you see Willa becoming stronger by dealing with the difficult things in her life? Do you believe that our struggles in life make us stronger? Why or why not?
4. Willa had a hard time dealing with her mother's death. She talked to Meg about it, then Marc, her dad, and even a therapist. Marc had hard things to deal with too. Why do you think it's good to talk about our problems and feelings with others? If you had a difficult problem, who would you talk to? Why?

5. Willa tried out for the swim team, trying to get closer to Marc. What do you do with your friends? Why might it be good to try new things?

6. For most of this book, Willa thought that Lizzy was her enemy. Willa was wrong. Have you ever misjudged someone? What do you think we can do to avoid misjudging other people?

7. How are Willa and Marc similar? How are they different? Willa is also friends with people who are older and younger than she is. Can you name some examples? Why do you think it is important to be friends with different kinds of people?